KT-513-568

EX LIBRIS
VINTAGE CLASSICS

TWENTY THOUSAND LEAGUES UNDER THE SEA

Jules Verne was born on February 8, 1828, in the city of Nantes, France. He is best known for his novels *A Journey to the Centre of the Earth*, *Twenty Thousand Leagues Under the Sea*, *The Mysterious Island* and *Around the World in 80 Days*. Verne is often referred to as the 'Father of science fiction' because he wrote about space, air and underwater travel before aeroplanes, spacecrafts and submarines were invented. He died in 1905.

OTHER WORKS BY JULES VERNE

Paris in the 20th Century

Journey to the Centre of the Earth

From the Earth to the Moon

The Adventures of Captain Hatteras

In Search of the Castaways

Around the Moon

Around the World in 80 Days

The Mysterious Island

The Blockade Runners

The Green Ray

Facing the Flag

The Lighthouse at the End of the World

JULES VERNE

Twenty Thousand Leagues Under the Sea

TRANSLATED FROM THE FRENCH BY
James Reeves

VINTAGE BOOKS
London

Published by Vintage 2011

2 4 6 8 10 9 7 5 3 1

Twenty Thousand Leagues Under the Sea was first published in France as *Vingt mille lieues sous les mers* in 1869

This edition first published by Beaver Books in 1956 and by Chatto & Windus in 1969

Vintage
Random House, 20 Vauxhall Bridge Road,
London SW1V 2SA

www.vintage-classics.info

Addresses for companies within The Random House Group Limited can be found at: www.randomhouse.co.uk/offices.htm

The Random House Group Limited Reg. No. 954009

A CIP catalogue record for this book is available from the British Library

ISBN 9780099528531

The Random House Group Limited supports The Forest Stewardship Council (FSC), the leading international forest certification organisation. All our titles that are printed on Greenpeace approved FSC certified paper carry the FSC logo. Our paper procurement policy can be found at: www.randomhouse.co.uk/environment

Mixed Sources
Product group from well-managed forests and other controlled sources
www.fsc.org Cert no. TT-COC-002139
© 1996 Forest Stewardship Council

Printed and bound in Great Britain by
CPI Bookmarque, Croydon CR0 4TD

Contents

Twenty Thousand Leagues Under the Sea

1

Professor Aronnax Is Invited to Join a Monster-Hunt

In the year 1867 I had been on an expedition to collect plants and animals in the bad lands of Nebraska in North America. I was a professor in the Paris Museum of Natural History. While I was in New York, on my way home to France, a mysterious accident happened to the Cunard liner *Scotia*. She was steaming along peacefully in mid-Atlantic, when she was suddenly struck by something sharp, and the stokers rushed up on deck shouting that the ship was sinking. A hole about two yards wide was found in her side, and as it was impossible to stop such a large leak, she had to limp home to Liverpool with her paddles half under water. They got her into dry dock, and the engineers could hardly believe their eyes when they found a triangular hole in the armour-plating, so neat that it might have been bored by machinery.

All New York was buzzing with the story, which was indeed only the latest of a great number of strange happenings which had been going on at sea for nearly a year. Ships had told of meeting 'an enormous thing' in the sea, a long, cigar-shaped object, shining in the dark, very much larger and faster than a whale. Some of the crews were certainly going too far when they said it was a mile wide and three miles long, yet it was clear that the strange being was very much larger than any kind of whale known to man. One captain thought he had come across an unknown reef off the coast of Australia, and just as he was getting ready to mark its position on his chart, he saw two spouts of water shooting up a hundred and fifty feet into the air. This made him think that it was a huge whale, spouting through its blowholes. Other ships saw the same sort of thing, and the strangest part of it all was that the monster was sighted at widely distant parts of the ocean with only a few days' time between, which meant that it must be able to move with terrific speed.

Newspapers all over the world started printing stories about the monster, and talked of sea serpents and other strange beasts. And it was not only the newspapermen who were excited, but the professors and men of science. They agreed in the end that the thing could not be a floating reef or island, since it moved so quickly, but could only be either an enormous whale, or else a very powerful submarine. This last idea was most disturbing, because only the government of a country could possibly be rich and powerful enough to build such a machine secretly. But enquiries were made in England, France, Russia, Prussia, Spain, Italy, America, and even in Turkey, and all the governments said that they knew nothing about such a vessel, so the idea of a submarine had to be given up.

When I arrived in New York, several people asked me what I thought about it all. I had written a book called *The Mysteries of the Great Depths of the Sea*, so they thought I ought to know something about the matter. In the end, I wrote a story for the *New York Herald*, saying that in my view, the monster must be an enormous narwhal, or sea-unicorn, which is a creature of the whale family with a long tusk as hard as steel sticking out from its snout. Although we have never heard of a narwhal longer than about sixty feet, and this one appeared to be about three hundred feet long, it might perhaps be a creature left over from an early age of the world. We know that there were once huge land animals, very much larger than modern elephants, so why not also sea-monsters?

My newspaper article was considered very good, but in the meantime people all over the world were becoming seriously frightened. All shipwrecks which had no known cause were put down to the work of the creature, and there was a general outcry to rid the seas of the terrible beast.

The Americans were the first in the field, and they decided to send out an expedition to hunt down the monster. A fast frigate of the American Navy, the *Abraham Lincoln*, was put in commission, under the orders of Commander Farragut, who hastened to fit her out with arms and ammunition. Then, when the ship was ready, they did not know where to send her, as nothing had been heard of the animal for two months. Suddenly there was a report that it had just been seen in the North Pacific, and the ship was ordered to sail within twenty-four hours. All was made ready, she was stocked with food and coal, and the crew were signed on.

Three hours before she sailed, a page boy came to me in my hotel.

'Professor Aronnax? Letter for you, sir.'

I took the letter. It was from the Secretary of the United States Navy, and invited me to join the expedition.

2

My Man Counsel

Before the letter came, I had no more idea of hunting the monster than of flying to the moon, but as soon as I had read it, that was the only thing in the world I wanted to do. I had been longing to get back home, to see my country and my people again, to say nothing of my little flat in the Zoo and my beloved collections. But the letter put all that out of my head, and I accepted the invitation without another thought.

'Anyway,' I said to myself, 'perhaps we may be lucky enough to capture the animal in the European seas, and then I shall be able to take back at least half a yard of its ivory tusk for the Museum.' It would certainly be a long way round, to set out for France by way of the North Pacific.

'Counsel!' I cried impatiently.

Counsel was my servant, a brave Fleming and my devoted friend. He followed me on all my journeys, a good, quiet, regular fellow who was never surprised at anything. He was very clever with his hands, and ready to turn them to anything, and, in spite of his name, never giving any counsel whatever. He knew a great deal about plants and animals from books, but very little from real life. He had been with me for ten years, and would follow me to China or the Congo without turning a hair. He had only one fault, and that was that he was so extremely polite that it sometimes got on my nerves. He would never speak to me directly – for instance, he would never say, 'Shall I come with you?' but always, 'Does the master wish me to come with him?'

'Counsel!' I shouted again, and started packing wildly. If it had been an ordinary journey, I should never have dreamed of asking him if he wanted to come with me, but this was a desperate enterprise, in chase of a monster which could upset a frigate as easily as a walnut shell, and I wanted to know what he thought about it. Counsel came in.

'Did the master call?'

'Yes, my boy. Pack our things, we're leaving in two hours!'

'As the master pleases,' he replied calmly.

'Not a second to lose! Stuff everything into my trunk, all my travelling things, and as many coats, shirts and socks as you can get in, quick!'

'And the master's collections?' said Counsel.

'We'll see about them later.'

'What! All the master's beautiful stuffed animals!'

'We can leave them at the hotel.'

'And the master's opossum?'

'They'll feed it for us. Anyway, I shall get them to send all our animals home to France.'

'Then we're not going back to Paris?' asked Counsel.

'Why, yes, of course . . .' I answered, 'but we shall be making a sort of a loop.'

'Whatever loop the master pleases.'

'Oh, it won't be much! Not quite straight home, that's all. We're sailing in the *Abraham Lincoln*.'

'As it suits the master.'

'Well, you know what it is, Counsel, we're going to chase the monster! A glorious adventure – dangerous too! These monsters are rather tricky. But we're going! We've got a fine Captain!'

'I will do as the master does,' said Counsel.

'Now, are you quite sure you want to come? We may never come back, you know.'

'As the master pleases.'

The trunks were packed with lightning speed, I paid my bill, arranged for the collections to be sent to Paris and for the opossum to be looked after, then we jumped into a cab and were whirled through the streets of New York to the docks. When we arrived, we could see two great columns of black smoke coming from the funnels of the *Abraham Lincoln*.

We dashed on board. There I was introduced to Commander Farragut, who shook hands and welcomed me.

I had a comfortable cabin in the after part of the ship.

'We shall be very snug here,' I said to Counsel.

'As snug as a hermit-crab in a borrowed shell,' said he.

I left him unpacking our trunks, and went up on deck. I found the sailors just casting off the last moorings, so that if we had arrived only ten minutes later I should have missed that extraordinary, strange and improbable adventure which many people will hardly believe, even when I tell the true story.

The frigate moved down the river towards the sea, and the crowds on the banks gave us a fine send-off, cheering and waving their handkerchiefs. Then the ship passed between the forts, which fired a volley in salute from their biggest guns, and the *Abraham Lincoln* replied by hoisting the Stars and Stripes three times. At last the shores of America grew faint in the distance, and we were steaming at full speed through the dark waters of the Atlantic.

3

Ned Land the Harpooner

As soon as we were in the open sea, we began to keep a watch for the monster, though we were not yet in the Pacific. Commander Farragut offered a reward of two thousand dollars for the first man, cabin-boy, sailor or officer, who should catch sight of it. We all spent long hours in the rigging, scanning the sea. Only Counsel remained calm, and did not share in the general excitement.

The ship was fitted with all possible tackle for catching whales, from the simple harpoon thrown by hand to the latest kind of harpoon-gun. But best of all, she had in her crew Ned Land, the king of harpooners.

Ned Land was a Canadian, a very cool and cunning whaler. He was over six feet tall, and powerfully built, a grave and reserved man, but he could be very violent when provoked. He was worth the rest of the crew put together, for the keenness of his eyes and the strength of his arms. He came from Quebec, which used to belong to France, and as I was a Frenchman he came to be fond of me, and forgetting his usual silence he would tell me tales of his adventures with whales in the polar seas.

One fine evening, three weeks after the beginning of our voyage, I was sitting with Ned Land on the quarter-deck. We were drawing near to the Magellan Straits, and within a week we would be in the Pacific. We were looking out over the sea, talking of one thing and another, and I wanted to know what he thought about the monster. It seemed that he did not believe in it at all.

'Why ever not, Ned?' I asked him. 'You're a whaler, why don't you believe in this enormous whale?'

'It's just because I am a whaler, Professor Aronnax,' answered Ned. 'It's just because I do know something about whales that I can't believe this story. I've hunted hundreds of whales, I've harpooned a good few, I've killed quite a number, but I still can't believe there is such a thing as a whale that could make a hole in an armour-plated ship.'

'But, Ned, I've heard of whales making holes right through ships.'

'Wooden ships, perhaps, though I've never seen it. It can't be a whale. Perhaps a giant squid?'

'Not a squid, Ned. Their flesh isn't hard enough.' I went on for a long time, trying to make him admit that the creature must be a giant whale, but he stuck to his opinion that no whale of any kind could pierce an iron-clad ship, so in the end we left it at that.

4

The Monster at Last!

One day we came up with some American whale-boats, near the Falkland Islands, but they had not seen our animal. The captain of one of these boats, knowing that Ned Land was on board, asked for his help in hunting a whale they had in sight. Commander Farragut, wishing to see Ned at work, willingly let him go, and he had the good fortune to strike two whales. After this, no one had any doubts who would be the victor if the narwhal should come within range of Ned's harpoon.

The frigate had made great speed down the coast of South America, and at last we rounded Cape Horn. We were in the Pacific!

'Keep your eyes skinned, boys!' shouted the men. Eyes were glued to telescopes, and took no rest. Perhaps they were rather dazzled by the hope of the two thousand dollars reward. Day and night the sailors scanned the sea. And I too, although the bait of the money did not tempt me, spent nearly all my time on deck, caring for neither sun nor shower, taking only a few minutes off for my meals, a few hours for sleep. How many times were we wildly excited for a false alarm, when someone caught sight of the black back of a whale above the waves! The whole crew swarmed up on deck, and I looked till I could hardly see, while Counsel said to me calmly,

'If the master did not strain his eyes with looking, he would see much better.'

Ned Land still refused to believe in the creature, he did not even bother to look at the sea, except during his watch. The stubborn Canadian spent eight hours out of twelve reading or sleeping in his cabin. This annoyed me, because he had such powerful sight that he could have been a great help.

'Bah!' said he, 'there's nothing to see, Mr Aronnax, or if there is some creature, what chance have we of ever sighting it? They say it's been seen in the Pacific, but, from all accounts, this narwhal isn't one to moulder for long in the same quarters. Here today, gone tomorrow, that's our beast, if there is such a thing.'

On July 27th, we crossed the Equator, and the frigate headed west, towards the China seas. This was the area where the creature had last been seen, and excitement on board rose to fever pitch. The crew neither ate nor slept, and twenty times a day our hopes were raised by the cry of the look-out in the crow's nest who thought he had seen the beast.

After all these false alarms the crew lost heart in the end. For three months they had watched the deserted seas, and had caught never a glimpse of anything out of the ordinary. They wanted to give up and go home. At last they put it to Commander Farragut, who agreed that if the monster had not been sighted within three days he would put the helm about and return to America.

Two days passed, and everything possible was done to attract the creature, if it should happen to be in those waters. Huge sides of bacon were trailed after the ship, to the great delight of the sharks. Night was falling, next day the Commander would keep his promise and return. I was leaning over the side, with Counsel beside me, and the men were still watching the water through the growing darkness. For the first time, I thought, Counsel seemed to be sharing in the general excitement.

'Well, Counsel,' I said, 'here's your last chance of pocketing two thousand dollars.'

'I hope the master realises,' said he, 'that I have never set my heart on any reward, and that the United States Government would never be the poorer for me.'

'You're quite right, Counsel. What a stupid affair, after all, so much excitement for nothing. We might have been back in France, six months ago . . .'

'In the master's little flat in the Museum,' he answered; 'and the collections would be arranged, and the master's opossum would be in his cage in the Zoo, drawing great crowds!'

'As you say, Counsel, and of course I suppose everyone will laugh at us!'

'Certainly,' he went on calmly, 'I think they will laugh at the master. And . . . should I go on?'

'Go on, Counsel.'

'Well, the master will only get what he deserves!'

'Really!'

'When a gentleman has the honour to be a professor like the master, he should not do things that will make people . . .'

Counsel had no time to finish. A voice rang out of the silence. It was Ned Land.

'Ahoy there!' he cried, 'the Thing! On our weather beam!'

5

The Chase

At this cry, the whole ship's company rushed towards Ned Land – the Commander, officers, petty officers, sailors, cabin-boys – even the engineers left their engines and the stokers their fires. The engines were stopped, and the ship drifted. By then the darkness was complete, and I wondered how the Canadian could have seen anything, however good his eyes were. My heart was beating wildly.

But Ned had made no mistake, and we could all see the thing he was pointing at. Two cables from the *Abraham Lincoln*, on her starboard beam, the sea seemed to be lit up from below. The monster was lying several fathoms under the surface of the water, and threw out an intense and brilliant light. This was in the shape of an enormously long and very narrow oval, much brighter in the middle and getting fainter towards the ends.

'It's nothing but a luminous stretch of the sea,' said one of the officers.

'No, sir,' I exclaimed, 'it's far too bright for that, it's some sort of electric light. And look! it's moving! it's coming towards us!' There was a general cry.

'Quiet there!' said Commander Farragut. 'Up with the helm! Engines hard astern!' A man rushed to the wheel, the engineers to the engines. The ship moved astern in a half circle.

'Starboard the helm! Full speed ahead!' cried the Commander. The frigate moved quickly from the light – that is, she tried to move away, but the strange animal came on with a speed double that of the ship.

We were breathless. Astonishment rather than fear kept us still and silent. The animal was playing with us, it circled round the frigate and wrapped her in a luminous mist. Then it made off for two or three miles, leaving a trail of light like torrents of steam from an express train. Suddenly the creature shot towards the ship with terrifying speed, stopped dead twenty feet from us, and went out. The brightness suddenly stopped as if turned off. Then it appeared again on the other side of the ship, and we did not know if it had circled round her or slid under the keel. At any minute there might have been a collision which would have been the end of us.

I was astonished when I saw that the frigate was running away from the creature and not trying to attack, and I spoke to the Commander about it.

'Mr Aronnax,' he answered, 'I don't want to risk my ship in the darkness against an unknown enemy. Wait till daylight, then I shall attack.'

'You think you know now, sir, what sort of creature it is?'

'Yes, it's certainly a gigantic narwhal, and an electric one, too.'

'In that case,' I said, 'we can't get near it, any more than a torpedo-fish or an electric eel.'

'It may easily be able to give an electric shock like a flash of lightning, so you can see we must keep good watch.'

No one thought of sleep that night. The ship was no match for the narwhal in speed, and she was kept moving slowly. The animal stayed nearby, rocking in the waves. However, about midnight it disappeared, or rather it went out like a great glowworm. We did not know whether it had fled or not. Then suddenly a loud whistling sound was heard like water forced out violently. At that time I was on the quarter-deck with the Commander and Ned Land.

'Ned' said the Commander, 'you've often heard whales bellowing?'

'Often, sir, but never such a whale as has just earned me two thousand dollars.'

'You've a right to your reward. But tell me, wasn't that noise like a whale spouting through its blowholes?'

'Just the same, sir, only this one was enormously louder. I'm sure now, though, it must be a whale down there in the water. If you'll allow me, sir, I'll have a little talk with it tomorrow morning.'

'If it's in the mood to listen to you, Master Land,' I said.

'Just let me get within four harpoons' length of it,' said Ned, 'and we'll see if it'll listen to me!'

'But to get near to it,' said the Commander, 'must I lend you a whale-boat?'

'Of course, sir.'

'And risk the lives of my men?'

'And mine,' said the harpooner simply.

About two o'clock in the morning the light shone out again, as brightly as before, about five miles from the ship. In spite of the distance, and the noise of the wind and the sea, we could hear quite clearly the strong beating of the animal's tail, and even its panting breath.

'Hum!' I thought, 'a whale with the strength of a cavalry regiment would be a very fine whale!'

When the day began to break we prepared for battle. The harpoon-guns were got ready, and Ned Land sharpened his hand-weapon. The electric light from the narwhal went out with the dawn, and by seven o'clock it was daylight, though there was a very thick morning mist. At eight o'clock, the fog began to lift, and suddenly, as on the night before, we heard Ned's voice:

'There it is! To port, astern!'

There, a mile and a half from the ship, a long dark body rose about a yard above the waves. Its tail was beating violently and a great white wake marked its course. The frigate drew nearer to the whale. I had a good look at the animal, and it seemed to me that it was not quite as long as had been reported – not more than about two hundred and fifty feet. While I was watching, two jets of steam and water shot out from its blowholes to a height of about forty feet.

The crew were eagerly waiting for the orders of the chief. Commander Farragut, after looking at the animal carefully, called for the chief engineer.

'Have you plenty of steam?' he asked.

'Yes, sir,' said the engineer.

'Good. Stoke up, then, and put her full ahead!'

Three cheers greeted this order. It was the hour of battle. The ship's two funnels shot out torrents of black smoke, and the deck trembled with the thrust of the pistons. The powerful screw drove the ship forward towards the monster, who allowed us to come within half a cable, then started moving away, keeping the same distance. The chase went on for about three-quarters of an hour, but the frigate got no nearer to the whale. We would never catch it up at that rate.

Commander Farragut twisted his shaggy beard in rage.

'Ned Land!' he cried. 'Do you advise me to lower the whale-boats?'

'No, sir,' said Ned, 'that beast won't let itself be caught unless it chooses.'

'Then what?'

'Force steam if you can, sir, and if you'll allow me, I'll post myself on the bowsprit. Then, if we get within a harpoon's length, I'll throw.'

'Go ahead, then. Engineer, more steam!'

Ned went to his post. The fires were stoked still higher, the frigate steamed ahead at fifteen knots. She kept up the pace for over an hour, without gaining on the whale. The crew were growing angry, and started swearing at the monster, who took no notice at all. Commander Farragut was biting his beard now, he called the engineer again, and called, 'Engineer, screw down the safety valves!'

'Counsel,' I said, 'I suppose you know we shall probably blow up?'

'As the master pleases!' said Counsel. But I must admit that I was rather thrilled by the risk.

We put on still more speed, till we were making over sixteen knots, but the whale kept its distance without turning a hair. What a chase! We were all keyed up with the excitement. Ned Land kept at his post, harpoon in hand. Several times, the animal allowed us to draw nearer.

'We're winning! we're winning!' cried the Canadian. But just as he made ready to throw the harpoon, the whale made off at about twenty-five knots. A cry of fury rose from the whole crew.

Commander Farragut decided to take more direct action, and ordered the fo'c'sle gun to be loaded and aimed. The shell passed a few feet over the whale, which was about half a mile away.

'Let a better man try!' cried the Commander, 'and five hundred dollars to the man who hits the infernal brute!'

An old grey-bearded gunner, calm and cool, went up to the

gun, levelled it and took steady aim. The shell hit the animal but slid off the smooth skin and buried itself far away in the sea.

The old gunner was furious. 'That's an armour-plated beast,' he cried.

'Devil take it!' cried the Commander, 'but I'll go on with the hunt till the ship blows up!'

The chase went on hour after hour till the sun went down, and darkness covered the sea. I thought we had lost the strange animal, and would never see it again, but I was wrong. About eleven o'clock, the electric light shone out again three miles to windward, as brilliant as on the night before. The narwhal seemed to be quiet, perhaps asleep in the waves, tired out by the day's chase. Ned Land, who had often harpooned sleeping whales, took up his post again on the bowsprit. The frigate came up quietly, the engines were stopped two cables from the animal, and the ship drifted. The decks were silent, we hardly breathed. We were a hundred feet from the monster, the light dazzled our eyes. At that moment, leaning on the fo'c'sle rail, I saw Ned Land below me, clinging on with one hand, with the other brandishing his terrible harpoon. He was scarcely twenty feet from the quiet animal. Suddenly his arm shot out violently, then I heard a dull clang from the harpoon as it struck.

The electric light went out at once, and two great water-spouts thundered on to the deck, rushing in a torrent from stem to stern, knocking down men, tearing the lashings apart. There was a terrible shock, and I was thrown over the rail into the sea.

6

A Whale of Unknown Kind

When I was first shot into the sea, I sank for about twenty feet. But I am a good swimmer, and did not lose my head, and two hard kicks brought me up to the surface again. I looked for the ship – had anyone seen me vanish? Would they put out a boat to save me? The darkness was deep, but I could make out the vague shape of the ship disappearing towards the east, its signal lights fading in the distance. I felt I was lost.

'Help! Help!' I cried, swimming desperately towards the *Abraham Lincoln*. My clothes clung to my body, strangling my movements. I was sinking, I could not breathe.

'Help!' It was my last cry, my mouth filled with water, I struggled, dragged down into the depth.

Suddenly my clothes were seized by a strong hand, I was pulled violently back to the surface, and I heard these words in my ear,

'If the master would have the great kindness to lean on my shoulder, the master would swim much more easily!'

I caught my faithful Counsel by the arm. 'You!' I said. 'You!'

'Myself,' said Counsel, 'at the master's service.'

'You were washed overboard too?'

'Not at all, sir, but since I am at the master's service, I followed.' He thought that quite natural.

'And the ship?' I asked.

'The ship!' said Counsel, turning on his back. 'I think the master would do well to forget about the ship!'

'What do you mean?'

'Only that, as I jumped into the sea, I heard the helmsman crying that the screw and the rudder were smashed!'

'Smashed?'

'Yes, by the monster's teeth. I think that was the only damage to the ship, but unfortunately for us, she can't steer.'

'Then we're lost!'

'Perhaps,' said Counsel calmly. 'However, we still have several hours before us, and many things can happen in several hours.'

My servant's unruffled calm gave me courage, and I struck out boldly. But I was weighed down by my clothes which felt like a cloak of lead. Counsel noticed this.

'If the master will allow me to make a cut?' he said. He slid a knife under my clothes and slit them quickly from top to toe. Then he slipped them off me, while I swam for the two of us. I did the same for him, and we went on swimming. We decided that our only hope would be if the ship had sent out a boat to pick us up, and Counsel worked out a plan for us to keep afloat as long as possible. We took it in turns to lie flat on the water, while the other swam and pushed his companion along. In this way we saved our strength as far as we could, and hoped we should be able to keep afloat till daylight.

So we went on, but at last I was seized by violent cramp. Counsel had to hold me up, and I could hear him panting.

'Leave me!' I told him.

'Leave the master?' he cried. 'Never! I shall drown before him!'

At that moment the moon appeared from behind a great cloud, and the sea shone. I could see the ship, five miles away, but not a sign of a boat. I tried to cry out, though the ship was too far to hear us, but I could not utter a sound through my swollen lips. Counsel could still speak, and cried 'Help! Help!'

We listened, and it seemed to me that there was a faint reply.

'Did you hear?' I whispered.

'Yes! Yes!' And he cried out again, desperately.

This time, there was no mistake. A human voice answered us. Was it another victim of the collision, or a voice from a boat hailing us in the darkness?

Counsel managed to hoist himself up a little in the water, leaning on my shoulder, then sank back exhausted.

'What did you see?'

'I saw . . .' he gasped, 'I saw . . . but we won't speak . . . keep our strength!'

What could he have seen? I don't know why, but for the first time I thought of the monster. But the human voice? There are no Jonahs in our time. We went on, Counsel still towing me. Sometimes he cried out, and the answering voice sounded nearer. I could hardly hear. I was at the last gasp, my fingers could not keep their hold any longer, my mouth was filled with salt water, the cold numbed my body.

Suddenly I was struck by something hard, and I clung to it. I was pulled out of the water, then I fainted. I came back to my senses with the feeling that someone was rubbing me vigorously.

'Counsel,' I murmured.

'Did the master ring?' said he. At that moment, by the last light of the setting moon, I saw another figure.

'Ned!' I cried.

'Myself, sir,' he said, 'and still in chase of my reward!'

'You too were thrown into the sea by the collision?'

'Yes, Professor, but I had better luck than you. I managed to land almost at once on a floating island.'

'An island?'

'Or, if you like, on your gigantic narwhal.'

'Explain, Ned.'

'Well, I found out soon enough why my harpoon wouldn't stick.'

'Why, Ned?'

'For the simple reason, dear Professor, that the beast is made of armour plate.'

I was startled by these words, and began to have a closer look at our island. I felt the surface, and found it much harder than any whale. Perhaps it could be some beast with hard scales like a tortoise? But no, the shining, polished surface clanged when it was struck. The sea-monster which had been puzzling scientists and sailors all over the world turned out to be something even more wonderful than anyone had believed possible. It was man-made, a gigantic submarine, like a steel fish.

'Then,' I said, 'it must have some sort of mechanical power, and a crew to manage it?'

'Certainly it must,' said the harpooner, 'but during the three hours I've been here it hasn't moved. It's just been rocking in the waves.'

'Well anyway,' I went on, 'there must be someone on board, so we're saved!'

'Hum!' said Ned in a doubtful tone.

Just then there was a bubbling noise at the stern of the strange craft, and it started to move forward. We clung on to the top, which was about a yard above the water, and luckily the speed was not very great.

'As long as she keeps on the level,' murmured Ned, 'I've no complaints. But if she takes it into her head to dive, I wouldn't give two bucks for my skin!'

Ned was right. I searched all over the surface for some kind of manhole, but there was no sign of anything of the sort. We could do nothing. We were making towards the west, and I reckon our speed was about ten knots. The moon had set and it was quite dark, except when phosphorescent water shot up from the propeller. About four o'clock in the morning, the speed increased, the waves whipped us, and we had great difficulty in holding on.

Luckily Ned found a wide anchor-ring fixed to the armour-plating, and we managed to cling to that.

It was a long night, but at last the day dawned. When the morning mist cleared, I started to inspect the hull carefully, especially a sort of level deck on top. Suddenly I felt it slowly sinking.

'A thousand devils!' cried Ned Land, kicking the metal, 'open up there, confound you!' But his voice was lost in the beating of the screw.

Suddenly there was a clanging noise from inside the boat, and a hatch was lifted. A man appeared, and disappeared at once with a strange cry. A few seconds later, eight strong men with masked faces appeared silently, and drew us down into their amazing machine.

7

On Board the Submarine

We were carried off like lightning. I don't know what the others thought when we were forced into this floating prison, but the blood froze in my veins. Who were our captors? Certainly a new kind of pirate.

As soon as the hatch was shut, it was completely dark. I felt the treads of an iron ladder under my bare feet. Ned and Counsel followed, held in an iron grasp. At the foot of the ladder, a door opened and closed at once upon us with a metallic sound. We were alone. Where? I had no idea, it was completely black.

Ned Land was furious. 'A thousand devils!' he cried, 'these people are savages! They're probably cannibals. But I'll certainly kick up a row if they want to eat me!'

'Keep calm, Ned,' said Counsel. 'Don't get excited. We're not in the baking-tin yet!'

'No, but we're certainly in the oven, it's as black as pitch! Luckily I still have my knife, and I don't need much light to use that. The first of these bandits who lays hand on me . . .'

'Don't shout so, Ned,' I told him. 'Maybe they can hear us. Let's see if we can find out where we are.'

I started to feel round our prison. After a few steps I came up against an iron wall, then I bumped into a wooden table and several stools. There was thick matting on the floor, but I could find no openings. After about half an hour, our prison was suddenly lit up brilliantly. I blinked, then saw that the light came from an electric globe above our heads.

'Light at last!' cried Ned, waving his knife.

I took a good look round the cabin. There was nothing in it but the table and five stools, the door was invisible in the iron-plated walls. Not a sound could be heard, we had no idea whether we were on the surface of the ocean, or deep underneath it. But surely the light meant that someone was coming to see us?

Suddenly there was the noise of bolts being shot back, the door opened, and two men came in. The first was a little man, very strong, with broad shoulders, black shaggy hair, a thick moustache, and bright, sparkling eyes. He looked like a Southerner, from one of the Latin countries.

The second, however, was clearly the leader. I recognised him at once as a man of very strong character, calm, active, and brave. He held himself proudly, his black eyes looked at us with cold confidence, his face was pale, and there was a look of nobility about him. He was tall, with a broad forehead, fine features, and long, sensitive hands, such as go with a passionate nature. I was sure that he was the finest man I had ever seen. One particular thing I noticed about him was that his eyes, set rather far apart, could see almost a quarter of the horizon at once. I found out later that his power of sight was even greater than Ned Land's. When he looked at anything he frowned and his look was like a burning-glass. How he looked! Distant things grew nearer, as if his eyes were telescopes, and when he looked at you he saw into your very soul. His eyes saw through the water, so thick and muddy to us, and he read the secrets of the deepest seas.

The two strangers were wearing caps made of sea-otter fur, sealskin boots, and clothes of some strange stuff I did not recognise.

The captain looked at us without a word. Then he turned to his companion and spoke with him in a language I did not recognise. The other shook his head, and turned to me as if questioning me.

I replied (in French) that I did not understand, then Counsel suggested that I should tell them our whole story. So I told them everything that had happened, speaking very clearly, and not forgetting anything. I gave them our names and explained who we were.

The man with the calm and gentle eyes listened to me quietly, politely even, and with great attention, but he made no sign that he understood. When I had finished he said not a word, so I asked Ned to try English.

Ned's story was the same as mine, except that he got very excited and complained of our treatment, adding that we were dying of hunger. But our visitors didn't seem to understand English either; when he had finished they didn't bat an eyelid. Then Counsel told the whole story again in German, but with no better success.

After that, I racked my brains for my schoolboy Latin, and managed to stumble through the whole thing again. It was no good. The strangers exchanged several words in their incomprehensible tongue, and went away, without making any sign to us. The door closed behind them.

'This is the end!' cried Ned in fury. 'These people don't know any civilised lingo!'

'Don't get worked up, Ned,' I replied. 'Getting angry won't help us at all.'

'But, Professor,' he went on, 'we shall die of hunger in this iron cage! And even if they don't follow our words, we explained perfectly well that we wanted food. In any country in the world, if you open your mouth and make signs of munching, even a fool can tell you're dying of hunger.'

As he spoke, the door opened. A steward came in, carrying sea-coats and trousers, made of some strange material. While we were putting them on, the man was laying the table.

'That looks more like it,' said Counsel.

'Bah!' said the bad-tempered harpooner, 'what the devil do you think they'll give us for breakfast? Turtle's liver, fillet of shark, dogfish steak!'

'We shall see!' said Counsel. The dishes, under silver dish-covers, were placed neatly on the cloth, and we sat down. Certainly, these people were civilised, and, except for the electric light, I might have thought myself in one of the best hotels in Paris. There was neither bread nor wine. The water was fresh and clear, but it was only water, which did not please Ned at all. Among the dishes I recognised several kinds of fish, delicately prepared, but I had no idea what some of the food was, whether animal or vegetable, though it was all delicious. The table silver and china were very elegant, and every piece bore the following device:

MOBILIS
N
IN MOBILI

'Moving in the moving water!' These words suited the submarine very well, and the letter N must be the initial of the mysterious captain.

After we had eaten heartily, Ned and Counsel lay down on

the matting, and were soon fast asleep. I was troubled for a time by thoughts of the strange things that were happening to us, and violent nightmares tormented me. Then at last I too fell asleep.

8

The Anger of Ned Land

I don't know how long I slept, but when I woke at last, my companions were still sleeping. The table had been cleared, but nothing else had changed in our prison. I noticed only that it had become very stuffy, and I found some difficulty in breathing. I began to wonder what the submarine did to renew her supply of oxygen, when suddenly I was refreshed by a draught of good sweet fresh air, smelling of the sea. I soon found that the air was coming from a ventilator above the door.

The fresh draught woke Ned and Counsel, who sat up, rubbing their eyes.

'The master has slept well?' said Counsel, with his usual politeness.

'Very well, my boy,' I replied. 'And you, Ned?'

'Like a top. But I believe I can smell a sea breeze?'

I explained what had happened while they were asleep.

'Then that's the answer to the roaring we heard, when we thought this ship was a narwhal,' said the harpooner.

'Yes, of course, it was the breathing of the beast!'

'Anyway, Professor,' said Ned, 'I have no idea of the time,

but I'm sure it must be dinner-time!'

'Rather breakfast-time,' I answered, 'for I think we must have slept for twenty-four hours!'

'I don't care what meal it is,' said Ned, 'as long as it's food!'

Then Ned started working himself up again into a terrible rage, while Counsel and I tried to calm him.

'How long do you think these pirates are going to keep us in this iron box?' said Ned.

'I've no more idea than you. But it seems likely that our happening on the secret of the submarine may be dangerous for us, very dangerous, perhaps.'

'Unless the captain makes us serve in his crew,' said Counsel, 'until . . .'

'Until such time as another ship, faster or more cunning than the *Abraham Lincoln*, captures this nest of pirates, and sends us along with the crew to swing at the end of her yard-arm!'

'Well, Ned,' I said, 'that may be, but in the meantime, we can do nothing, so it's useless to argue about it.'

'I don't agree, Professor,' Ned answered, 'I think we ought to do something about it.'

'Whatever can we do, Ned?'

'Escape.'

'How on earth!'

'Easy,' said he. 'I suppose there aren't more than about twenty men in the crew. All we have to do is to wait our chance and overpower them. I suppose two Frenchmen and a Canadian will be more than a match for them!'

I knew it was useless trying to argue with the stubborn harpooner, so I answered, 'Well, Ned, we must wait our chance. Only do try to keep quiet, or you'll give the whole show away.'

'I promise you, I'll be patient,' said he, but he didn't sound very patient.

After that, we fell silent. I myself thought that the crew must be very much larger than Ned imagined, and it seemed to me quite impossible that we could make ourselves masters of the ship. Ned started pacing the room like a wild beast, knocking on the walls and kicking them. Our hunger grew, there was no sign of the steward, and Ned's fury became wilder. He cried out, but there was no sound in the ship. Everything seemed dead. The silence was terrifying.

At last there was a noise outside. The door opened and the steward appeared. Before I could stop him, Ned leapt at the wretched man, knocked him down, and had him by the throat. Counsel was trying to loosen Ned's hands from his half-suffocated victim, and I was helping, when suddenly I was struck still by these words, spoken in French:

'Calm yourself, Mr Land, and you, Professor, please listen to me.'

9

The Man of the Seas

It was the captain. At these words, Ned Land got up at once. The steward, half strangled, staggered out of the room at a sign from his master. The captain was leaning against the table, his arms crossed, looking at us. There was a silence which none of us dared to break. Then the stranger spoke.

'Gentlemen,' he said, in a calm and steady voice, 'I can speak French, English, German, and Latin. I could therefore have answered you before, but I wanted to know you first. Your four stories agreed in the main, so I know what men you are, your names and business.'

He spoke French with no accent, but I did not feel him to be a countryman of mine. He went on, 'You must think that I have been a long time in coming to see you again. That was because I did not know what to do with you. It is very annoying to me that you have come to me, a man who has cut himself off from the world. You have come to trouble my life . . .'

'Against our will,' I said.

'Against your will?' said the stranger, in a louder voice. 'Was it against your will that you sailed in the *Abraham Lincoln*, a ship which has been hunting me throughout the seven seas? Was it against your will that your shells struck my ship? Was it against his will that Land struck her with his harpoon?'

He sounded angry, but I answered, 'Sir, I don't suppose you are aware of the arguments that have been going on about you through all America and Europe. There have been many accidents to ships, and the *Abraham Lincoln* was only trying to rid the seas of a powerful monster.'

The captain smiled. 'Mr Aronnax,' he said, 'dare you tell me that your frigate would not have hunted and shelled a submarine as well as a sea-monster?'

I didn't know what to say. 'You must see then, sir,' he went on, 'that I have the right to treat you as enemies. I hesitated for a long time. I was not obliged to take you on board. I could easily have put you back on deck, dived, and forgotten your existence. Was not that my right?'

'Perhaps the right of a savage,' I said, 'not that of a civilised man.'

'Professor,' he said sharply, 'I am not what you call a civilised man. I have broken with the whole world of men for reasons of my own. I do not obey the laws of society, and I forbid you ever to speak to me of them.'

A flash of anger and scorn lit up the stranger's eyes as he spoke, and I knew that some terrible thing had happened in this man's past. He had cut himself off from human laws, he was free, no ship could hunt him in the depths of the sea. Only God, and his conscience, if he had one, were his judges.

'I was uncertain,' he went on, 'but in the end I thought that you could do me no harm if I had pity on you. You may stay on board, and you will have your freedom in the ship, on one condition. You have only to give me your word that you will keep to this condition.'

'Speak, sir,' I answered. 'I suppose it is a condition that an honest man can accept.'

'Certainly. It's this. It may be that certain things will happen which will oblige me to shut you up for some hours or even days. As I don't wish to use violence, I ask you to obey me without question. Things may happen which are not for your eyes, and I want to make it impossible for you to see them. Do you accept this condition?'

I wondered what such things could be, which only outlaws might see.

'We accept,' I replied. 'But I should like to ask you one question.'

'Speak,' he said.

'You have said that we shall be free on board?'

'Completely free.'

'What do you mean by this freedom?'

'Freedom to come and go, to see everything that goes on – except on certain rare occasions – in short, the same liberty as we have ourselves.'

'You mean, then,' I said, 'the liberty every prisoner has, of walking round his prison! I'm afraid that is not enough for us.'

'It will have to be enough for you.'

'What, are we never to see our homes and our people again?'

'No, sir, never. But since to live among men is slavery, you will have far more freedom with us.'

'What's all this!' cried Ned. 'I shall never give my word not to try to escape!'

'I don't ask for *your* word, Mr Land,' said the captain coldly.

'Sir,' I exclaimed, 'you're going too far! This is cruelty!'

'No, it's mercy. You are my prisoners of war. I'm keeping you, when I could have you thrown back into the sea at a word. You have attacked me, you have surprised a secret which no man in the world should have known, the secret of my whole life. And you think I'm going to send you back into the world! Never. I must keep you, for my own safety.'

I could see that argument would be useless.

'So,' I said, 'the choice is quite simply between life and death?'

'Simply that.'

'My friends,' I said, 'there's no answer to that. But we have no duty to the captain of this ship.'

'None, sir,' answered the stranger. Then he went on, in a gentler voice, 'Now, let me finish what I have to say. Mr Aronnax, I have often read your book on the great depths of the sea. You have done as much as you could from dry land. But you don't know everything. You won't be sorry you have come with me, when I show you the wonderland of the seas. I intend to go round the world again, under the sea – perhaps my last voyage. You will see what no man has ever set eyes on before – for I and my friends do not count.'

His words excited me, in spite of myself.

'Captain,' I answered, 'we shan't forget that we are shipwrecked men and you have taken us on board. As for me, I'll try to forget my loss of liberty in seeing the new wonders of the ocean.' I thought he was going to take my hand, but he did not.

'One more question,' I said. 'What name may we call you by?'

'For you, sir,' he answered, 'I am Captain Nemo. For me, you are the passengers of the *Nautilus*.'

He called, and a steward came. He gave him his orders in their language, then he spoke to Ned and Counsel.

'There is a meal for you in your cabin,' he said. 'Please follow this man. And now, Mr Aronnax, our lunch is ready.' I followed Captain Nemo along a lighted passage-way, till we came to a second door, which led into the dining saloon. At each end of the room were high oak dressers, and on the shelves were costly porcelain and glass. China plates shone under a lighted ceiling, decorated with fine paintings. In the centre of the room was a table laid with a splendid service. The captain showed me my place.

'Sit down,' he said, 'and eat like a man who must be starving.'

The lunch consisted of sea food of all kinds, and certain delicacies which I didn't recognise. It was very good, though with a peculiar taste which I soon got used to. Captain Nemo looked at me, I asked no questions, but he read my thoughts.

'Most of this food is unknown to you,' he said, 'but you can eat without fear. For a long time I have done without supplies from the land, but I am none the worse for it. My crew are strong and fit, and we all eat the same food.'

'These things come entirely from the sea, then?'

'Certainly, the sea supplies all my needs. Sometimes I fish with trawls, sometimes I hunt game in the submarine forests.'

I looked at him with surprise. 'Fish from the sea I understand,' I said, 'but surely this is meat?' I pointed to some fillets on one of the dishes.

'Those are turtle steaks,' he said, 'and here are some dolphin's livers which you would take for pork. I have a very clever cook who makes wonderful preserves with all sorts of produce from the sea. Here is cream made from whale's milk, sweetened with sugar from the great wrack of the North Sea, and do taste this jam of sea-anemones which is just as good as any made from the most luscious fruit.' I tasted, more from curiosity than from appetite, while I listened to the captain's strange tales.

'The sea feeds me, Mr Aronnax,' he went on, 'and clothes me too. The stuff you are wearing is woven from byssus, which as you know is the filament which binds certain shells to the rocks, and it's dyed with purple from Mediterranean shell-fish. Your bed is made of the softest seaweed of the ocean, your pen will be of whalebone, your ink from the cuttle-fish. Everything comes to me from the sea as one day it will all return!'

'You love the sea, Captain.'

'Yes, I love the sea. It is everything. It covers seven-tenths of the globe, it is a vast desert where man is never alone, since it teems with living things. The sea doesn't belong to tyrants, they can still fight on the surface, but thirty feet below, their power ceases. Ah, only in the sea can I be a free man!' The captain grew silent suddenly, feeling that he had spoken too much. For a few moments he paced the room in great excitement. Then he grew calm again, and turned to me.

'Now, Professor,' he said, 'if you wish to see over the *Nautilus*, I'm at your service.'

10

The *Nautilus*

Captain Nemo rose, and I followed him through a double door into another large room. It was a library. The walls were lined with high bookshelves of black ebony, inlaid with copper, filled with books all bound alike. Under the shelves were comfortable divans covered with brown leather, and in the middle of the room was a huge table strewn with magazines and a few old newspapers. 'What a wonderful library, Captain!' I said. 'How amazing that it can go with you into the deepest seas! You must have at least six or seven thousand volumes . . .'

'Twelve thousand, Mr Aronnax. On the day the *Nautilus* made her first voyage, I bought my last books and newspapers, and since that time the world has ceased to think and write for me. Please make yourself at home here, and read what books you like.'

I thanked him, and started to look at the books. They were written in all languages, and were of many kinds – history, poetry, novels, and science, but chiefly science.

'This room is not only a library,' said the captain, 'it's also a smoking-room.'

'What! Do you smoke on board?'

'Certainly. Try this cigar, I think you'll like it.'

I took the cigar, which looked as if it were made of gold leaf, and lit it.

'It's excellent,' I said, 'but it's not tobacco.'

'No,' he answered, 'it comes from a sort of seaweed, rich in nicotine. Do you regret your Havanas now?'

'No, indeed.'

Then Captain Nemo opened another door, and we went into an immense, brilliantly lit gallery. It was a museum, filled with all sorts of beautiful things. About thirty pictures, by the greatest masters of the world, hung round the walls, and there were fine statues on pedestals in the corners of the room. An organ stood in an alcove, with volumes of music by the great composers lying on top.

In the middle of the gallery was a floodlit fountain, falling into a basin formed of a single vast shell, about six yards in circumference. All round the fountain there were glass cases in which were shown the rarest treasures of the sea, shells and plants of every kind, from every part of the world. In special cases there were necklaces of the most beautiful pearls, pink, green, blue, yellow, and black. Some of these were larger than a pigeon's egg, and of enormous value.

'You're a naturalist, Professor, these things interest you,' said the captain. 'For me, they have a further charm, since I picked them up with my own hands.'

'Captain,' I cried, 'this is a wonderful collection, better than you can find in any museum in Europe. But, to tell you the truth, I am most interested in the ship herself, in the motive power, and how it all works. These instruments on the wall – will you explain them to me?'

'I shall be only too pleased, Mr Aronnax. But first, let me show you your cabin.'

I followed him into the passage-way and we went forward. There I found, not a cabin, but a fine bedroom, very well furnished. I turned to thank my host.

'Your room is next to mine,' said he, opening a door, 'and mine opens on to the gallery we have just left.' I followed him into his cabin. It was a bare room, almost like a monk's cell. There was an iron bed, a work-table, a wash-stand, nothing comfortable, only the bare necessities.

Captain Nemo asked me to take a seat, and began to explain how his submarine worked. He had all the usual mariner's instruments, and some additional gear. There was a depth-gauge, and thermometers to measure the temperature of the different layers of water. But the power which drove the ship was electricity. This was very exciting to me, as at that time the use of this power in the world was only just beginning to be discovered. Captain Nemo made his electricity very cleverly by extracting sodium from sea-water, and he used coal mined under the sea to make the sodium piles. Electricity gave the *Nautilus* her heat, light, and movement, and also by means of powerful pumps the captain could store enough air to enable him to remain under water for a long time. There was also an electric clock, and a log which worked by electricity, for gauging the speed of the ship.

'Look,' said the captain, showing me the log, 'we're making fourteen knots at present.'

'It's marvellous,' I said, 'and I can see that this new power will take the place of wind, water and steam.'

'We haven't finished yet, Mr Aronnax,' said the captain, getting up, 'and if you'll follow me, we'll visit the after part of the *Nautilus*.'

Indeed, I had already seen all the fore part of the ship, which was composed of the rooms I have described, as well as an air tank. The doors in the bulkheads closed hermetically, so that they could be sealed if there should be a leak anywhere.

I followed the captain to the centre of the ship. There we found ourselves in a sort of well, with an iron ladder going up.

'This ladder leads to the boat,' he said.

'What! You have a boat?'

'Certainly, it's light and unsinkable, and is useful for fishing and pleasure.'

'When you want to use it, I suppose you have to surface?'

'Not at all. The boat is fixed by bolts into a well in the hull, and the ladder leads to a hatch in the submarine which is opposite a hatch in the boat. When I'm in the boat, I shut both hatches and undo the bolts, and the boat shoots up to the surface like a cork. Then I open the hatch in the deck, fix the mast, hoist the sail, or take my oars, and off I go.'

'But how do you get back?'

'I don't get back, the *Nautilus* comes to me. I have an electric cable from the boat to the submarine, and I just send a telegram.'

'What could be simpler?' said I, almost out of my mind with all these marvels.

When we had passed the ladder which led to the deck, I saw a cabin where Counsel and Ned Land were eating a fine meal with much gusto. Then we went into the galley, where the cooking was all electric. There also, sea-water was distilled to make fresh drinking-water. Next there was a washroom with hot and cold water. After that came the crew's quarters, but the door was closed, so that I could get no idea of the number of men on board.

The motor-room was aft. It was long, and divided into two parts, the first contained the electric piles, and the second, the motors which drove the screw. At her greatest speed, the ship could make forty-five knots.

'Captain Nemo,' I said, 'I am absolutely astonished at the speed of your ship, which I saw when I was in the *Abraham Lincoln*. But you have many other secrets – that of diving and surfacing, of seeing your way, of steering in all directions. Is it too much to ask you to explain all this to me?'

'Not at all,' said the captain, after a slight pause, 'since you are never to leave this submarine. Come into the gallery. That is my work-room, and there I will explain to you the operation of the *Nautilus*.'

11

Captain Nemo Explains His Submarine

When we were comfortably seated on a sofa in the gallery, smoking cigars, the captain showed me the plans of the submarine.

'You see, Mr Aronnax, she is seventy-five yards long, and her beam is eight and a half yards. She has two steel hulls, one inside the other, which give her great strength and resistance to shock.

'Inside the ship are large water-tanks. They are filled with water for diving, and pumped dry again for surfacing. There are extremely powerful electric pumps which can overcome the external water-pressure. By filling the tanks, I can dive to about a thousand fathoms, but if I want to visit the lowest depths of the ocean, I have yet another means. There are hydroplanes on either beam which can be sloped up or down, so you see that by their aid the ship will glide downwards, driven by the force of the screw.'

'Well done, Captain! But how can the man at the wheel see where he's going?'

'The wheel-house is a tower with glazed port-holes, jutting out from the deck, with telescopes let into the walls. At the after end of the deck, there is a powerful lamp which lights up the sea.'

'Well done again!' I cried. 'That explains the phosphorescence of the narwhal, which excited the scientists so much! By the way, can you tell me if the damage to the *Scotia*, which made such a flurry, was done by accident?'

'Quite by accident. I was moving a fathom below the surface when the collision took place. I saw, however, that no harm was done.'

'None at all, Captain. But your meeting with the *Abraham Lincoln*?'

'I'm sorry, Professor, for the damage to one of the best ships of the gallant American Navy, but I was attacked and I had to defend myself. All I did was to make it impossible for her to harm me, and she would have no difficulty in getting repaired at the next port.'

'Ah, Captain!' I said, 'your *Nautilus* is certainly a wonderful ship!' It was clear to me that he loved the submarine like a child. 'Tell me,' I went on, 'how was it possible for you to build her in secret?'

'Every one of her parts, Mr Aronnax, came to me from a different quarter of the globe. The keel was forged in France, the propeller shaft in London, the armour-plating at Liverpool, the propeller in Glasgow. The tanks were made in Paris, the motors in Germany, the bows in Sweden, the precision instruments in New York. And all these firms received their plans from me under different names.'

'But where did you put the whole thing together?'

'I set up my workshops on a desert island, in the middle of the sea. There I and my brave companions built our *Nautilus*. When we had finished, we burnt all traces of our work.'

'You must be enormously rich, sir?'

'Infinitely rich, Professor. I could pay the French National Debt without inconvenience.'

I took a long look at the strange man who talked in this way. Was he making a fool of me? Time would tell.

12

The Black River

'Now, Professor,' said the captain, 'I should like to fix the exact point of the start of our voyage. It's a quarter to noon, I'm going to surface.' He pressed an electric bell three times. The pumps began working, and the *Nautilus* surfaced. We went up the ladder and came on deck. I could see the boat, a slightly rounded form amidships. Fore and aft were two towers with lenses set in their walls, one for the helmsman, the other for the lamp.

It was a calm, still day with not a cloud in the sky. There was nothing in sight, not an island, not a reef, not a ship. Captain Nemo took his bearings by the sun, holding his sextant in a hand as still as marble.

'Noon,' he said. We went back to the gallery, and he worked out our position. 'Mr Aronnax,' he said, 'we are in longitude 137 degrees 15 minutes west.'

'By what meridian?' I asked quickly, hoping that his reply would give away his nationality.

'I have several chronometers,' he replied, 'regulated on the meridians of Paris, Greenwich and Washington. But, in your honour, I will use the Paris meridian.' His answer told me nothing. He went on: 'Our latitude is 30 degrees 7 minutes north, that is about three hundred miles from the coast of Japan. Today, November 8th, at noon, our under-water voyage of exploration begins.'

'God preserve us!' I answered.

'Now,' said he, 'I will leave you to your studies. I have set a course east-north-east at a hundred and fifty feet depth. The gallery is at your disposal, and I'll leave you.'

Left to myself, I remained for a long time deep in thought, wondering about the strange Captain Nemo and his secret. I would have given a great deal to understand his mystery. Then I looked at the vast globe on the table, and put my finger on the point where we were then moving.

The sea has its rivers as well as the land, special currents which can be recognised by their temperature and their colour, the Gulf Stream being the most famous. We were moving in one of these currents, which the Japanese call the Kuro-Scivo, or Black River. It is a warm stream coming from the Gulf of Bengal, very dark blue in colour. I was tracing its course on the globe, when Ned and Counsel appeared at the door of the gallery. They stood awestruck at the marvels before their eyes.

'Where are we, for heaven's sake?' cried the Canadian. 'In the Quebec museum?'

'Come in, friends,' I said, 'we're on board the *Nautilus*, twenty-five fathoms deep.'

'I must believe the master,' said Counsel, 'but really, this place is enough to flabbergast even a Fleming like me.'

'Have a good look, my boy, you can practise your natural history here.' Counsel needed no pressing, he was already wandering round the glass cases, murmuring scientific names.

In the meantime Ned was asking me about the captain, and I

told him all I knew, or rather all I didn't know. I asked him if he on his side had seen or heard anything.

'Seen nothing, heard nothing,' said he. 'I haven't even caught a glimpse of the crew. Do you think by chance the crew's electric too?'

'What an idea!'

'Well, I don't see why not. But tell me, Mr Aronnax, you're always so knowing, have you any idea how many men there are on board, ten, twenty, fifty, a hundred?'

'I've no idea, Ned, and believe me, you'd better give up all idea of seizing the *Nautilus* or of escaping. This ship is certainly one of the masterpieces of modern times, and I should be very sorry not to have seen her. Do keep your hair on, Ned, and try to see all that goes on round us.'

'See!' said the harpooner. 'But I can't see a thing, we'll never see anything in this armour-plated prison! We might as well be blind . . .'

As he spoke, we were suddenly plunged in utter darkness. The lighted ceiling was extinguished. We stood silent, wondering what might happen, when we heard a sliding noise.

'It's the end of the end!' said Ned.

Suddenly two brilliant oblongs of light appeared at either side of the gallery. The sea was lit up, we were separated from the water only by two glass plates. The water was illuminated all round the *Nautilus*. It was a wonderful sight, quite beyond my powers of description, as if we were gazing at liquid light. We glued ourselves to the windows, silent with amazement. Then Counsel said,

'You wanted to see, Ned, well, now you can see!'

'Curious! very curious!' said the Canadian, forgetting his anger. 'People would come a long way to see this sight! But fish? I can't see any fish.'

'What does it matter to you,' said Counsel, 'since you wouldn't know what they were if you saw them.'

'I! A fisherman!' cried Ned. Then Counsel gave him a long lecture about all the different families of fish, but Ned was only interested in whether they were good to eat or not.

'Look!' said the harpooner, at the window, 'there are plenty of fish now! Tell me what they are.'

'I can't tell you,' said Counsel, 'that's my master's business.' Indeed the worthy fellow knew all about fish from books, but he was quite incapable of telling one from another when he saw them, while the Canadian named all the fish at once. The two of them together would have made a famous naturalist.

Then for two hours we stood at the windows, watching the fish as they passed. It was like an aquarium, except that the fish were free. There were whole armies of them, beautiful living creatures of all colours, shapes and sizes. They swarmed round the ship, drawn to the light like moths.

Suddenly the lights came on in the gallery. The steel shutters closed, the enchanting vision disappeared.

I thought Captain Nemo would come in, but he did not appear. It was five o'clock. Ned and Counsel went back to their cabin, and I returned to my room, where I found dinner ready.

After the meal, which consisted of turtle soup and various delicate fishes, I spent the evening quietly, reading, writing, and thinking. Then I slept deeply on my bed of sea-grass, while the *Nautilus* glided along the swift current of the Black River.

13

An Invitation By Letter

Two days passed without a sight of the captain, or of any of the crew. Ned, Counsel and I spent a good deal of the time together, wondering at the strange absence of our host.

The next morning, when I smelt the fresh sea air and knew that the *Nautilus* had surfaced, I went up on deck. It was six o'clock, and a grey, still day. I hoped I might meet the captain, but I saw no one but the man at the wheel. Sunrise came, tinting the clouds with lovely colours, and I sat on the hump of the boat, breathing the delicious air. I heard someone on the ladder. It was not the captain, but his first officer. He took no notice of me, but scanned the sea all round the horizon with a powerful telescope. Then he went to the hatch, and spoke some words, which I remember, as they were repeated every morning:

'Nautron respoc lorni virch.' I had not the faintest idea what they meant.

He disappeared down the hatch, and I followed him, thinking that the ship was going to dive.

Five days passed, and every morning I went on deck. I heard

the same man repeat the same words, but there was never a sign of the captain.

The next day I found a letter addressed to me on the table in my cabin. It was an invitation from the captain for me and my companions to join him in a hunting-party, which was to take place next morning in his forests of Crespo Island.

Ned and Counsel were beside me when I read the letter.

'A hunt!' cried Ned. 'Then the chap does make landfall sometimes.'

'So it would appear,' I said.

'Well, then,' said the Canadian, 'we'll accept. Once on dry land, we'll know what to do. Anyway, I shouldn't say no to a few slices of fresh venison.'

'Let's find Crespo Island on the map.' I looked at the globe, and found it was an islet, nothing but a little rock lost in the middle of the North Pacific.

'If he does land sometimes,' I exclaimed, 'he certainly chooses desert islands.'

The next day, when I awoke, I felt that the *Nautilus* was completely still. I dressed quickly, and went into the gallery. Captain Nemo was there, waiting for me. He rose and greeted me, and asked if we would like to go with him. He said nothing about his week's absence, so I didn't mention it either, I only said that we should like to join him in the hunt.

'But tell me, Captain,' I said, 'since you have nothing to do with the land now, how do you come to own forests in Crespo Island?'

'My forests never see the light of the sun, Professor,' he answered. 'They shelter no lions, tigers, panthers, or any other four-legged beast. They grow for me alone. They are submarine forests.'

'And are you going to take me to submarine forests?'

'Certainly.'

'On foot?'

'Yes, and without getting your feet wet either. And with a rifle in your hand.'

I looked at the captain in amazement. Certainly, his brain is touched, I thought. He has been in a fit of madness for a week, and hasn't recovered yet. What a pity!

The captain could see what I was thinking, but he only invited me to follow him into the dining-room, where breakfast was ready.

'Please join me at breakfast,' he said. 'We can talk as we eat. There's no restaurant in my forest, so you would do well to make a good meal now.'

I did as he suggested. There were fish, and some very tasty seaweeds. We drank water mixed with a fermented liquor made from another sort of seaweed. At first the captain ate without speaking, then he looked at me, and said,

'Mr Aronnax, you have been thinking I must be mad. You should not make such hasty judgements.'

'But, sir . . .'

'Let me explain. You know that men can work under water if they have suitable clothing and a supply of air is pumped to them.'

'You mean in diving gear,' I said.

'Yes. But the diver is not free, as he must have an air-line. If we had such lines, we couldn't go far from the *Nautilus*. I have a better way, which leaves me free. I carry on my back a steel tube of compressed air which is continually renewed by chemicals. There is a special filter which allows the air to come through at the ordinary pressure for breathing. My head is enclosed in a copper globe, such as divers wear. The air supply will last for nine or ten hours.'

'Splendid,' I said. 'But tell me, how can you see under water?'

'I have an electric lamp fastened to my belt.'

'You answer all my doubts, Captain. But the rifle? It must be an air-gun, to work under water.'

'Yes, it's a rifle worked by compressed air.'

'It must be very difficult to kill your quarry, as you have to fire through the water?'

'Not at all. The bullet has only to touch the animal to kill it. The bullets are electric, and explode like little bombs at the slightest shock. The rifle holds ten of them.'

'I have no more to say,' I answered. 'I'll come gladly.' He led me aft, and I called Ned and Counsel as we passed their cabin. Then we came to a sort of cell, near the motor-room, where we were to get into our diving-kit.

14

A Walk on the Bottom of the Sea

In this cell we saw a dozen diving-suits hanging on the wall. Ned scowled at the sight of them.

'But Ned, the forests of Crespo are submarine forests!'

'Fair enough,' said the harpooner gloomily, disappointed in his hope of fresh meat. 'What about you, Mr Aronnax, are you going to climb into that get-up?'

'Must do, Ned.'

'Do as you like,' said the harpooner, with a shrug, 'but I'm not getting into that rig unless I'm forced.'

'No one will force you, Ned,' said the captain.

'Is Counsel going to risk it?' asked Ned.

'I follow the master wherever he goes,' answered Counsel.

The captain called, and two men of the crew came to help us into the heavy suits, made of seamless rubber. The trousers ended in thick shoes, with heavy lead soles. The suit was reinforced by copper bands, to protect the body from the pressure of the water. The sleeves were joined to supple gloves.

Captain Nemo, Counsel and I were soon dressed in our diving-suits, as well as one of the crew, a giant of a man. We only had to put on our helmets. Before we did that, I asked to see the rifles. One of the crew gave me a gun, and I had a good look at its cunning mechanism.

'Captain,' I said, 'this is a fine rifle, I can hardly wait to try it! But how do we get to the bottom of the sea?'

'At this moment, Professor, the *Nautilus* is aground in five fathoms of water, and we can just walk away.'

'How do we get out?'

'You'll see.' The captain put on his helmet. Counsel and I did likewise, while Ned wished us 'Good hunting!' in a sarcastic tone. The helmet was screwed on to the copper collar which formed the top of the jacket. There were three windows in the helmet, made of thick glass. As soon as it was fixed, the compressed air apparatus began to work, and I found I could breathe easily.

I was so weighed down by all my gear that I could not move a step. But I felt myself pushed into a little room next door. My companions followed, the door closed on us, and we were in darkness. After a few minutes, I heard a loud whistling, and I felt cold rising from my feet upwards. It was clear that a valve had been opened, and the water was coming into the little room. When it was filled, a hatch opened in the side of the submarine, and there was a greenish light. The next minute we stepped out on to the bottom of the sea.

The captain walked in front, then Counsel and I together, while the sailor brought up the rear. My clothes no longer weighed me down, I could move quite easily. The light was very strong, I could see things clearly at a hundred feet, but in the distance they melted into a blue darkness. We were walking on a fine bed of level sand, which reflected the sun and shone brilliantly. For a quarter of an hour we walked on this shining sand, while the hull of the *Nautilus* grew faint in the distance.

But when night fell, her lamp would be lit to help us find our way back.

We walked on over the plain. I could see great rocks, covered with sponges and sea-anemones. It was ten o'clock, and as the sun slanted down into the water the light was broken up into all the colours of the rainbow. It was a magnificent sight, to see the underwater rocks, weed, shells, and sea-creatures stained with these brilliant colours.

Counsel and I loitered, like children in a field of flowers, but Captain Nemo beckoned us on. We left the sand behind, and came to a stretch of ooze, then to fields of seaweed. We walked through the weed and it floated round our heads in long streamers. It was nearly noon now, and the sun shone directly downwards into the water.

Now the ground sloped downwards, till we were fifteen fathoms deep. The rays of the sun became dim, we were in a reddish twilight. Then the captain stopped. He waited till I had come up with him, then pointed to some darker masses in the shadows a little way ahead.

'That must be the forest of Crespo Island,' I thought.

15

A Submarine Forest

This was Captain Nemo's kingdom, where he alone was master. The forest was made up of great tree-like plants, and as soon as we had made our way under the vast arcades I noticed a strange thing. All plants in that forest grew straight upwards, from the smallest weeds on the ground to the largest branches. They seemed to have stalks of iron. If I moved them aside with my hand they sprang back at once to their upright positions when I let them go.

There were sea-anemones on the ground, like flowers, and little fish swam through the branches like a swarm of humming-birds.

At about one o'clock, the captain called a halt. We lay down on a bed of weed, and were soon fast asleep. I don't know how long we slept, but when I woke, the captain was already on his feet. I was stretching myself, when I caught sight of something which made me jump up in a hurry.

A few feet away, a monster sea-spider, a yard high, was looking at me with evil eyes, ready to pounce. Although my diving-suit was thick enough to protect me against its bite, I drew back in horror. Counsel and the seaman woke up at that moment, and the captain pointed at the spider. The man struck it down with a blow of his rifle-butt, and I saw the claws of the monster writhing in terrible convulsions.

This meeting made me think that there might be other more fearsome creatures in these gloomy depths, and that my diving-suit would be no protection against them. So I kept on my guard.

We went on. The ground was still sinking, and at last we were in complete darkness. I was groping my way forwards, when suddenly a white light shone out. Captain Nemo had switched on his electric torch, and we all followed suit.

The trees were getting thinner now, but there were still a great many sea-creatures, anemones, molluscs, and fish of several kinds. I thought that our light would attract some sort of game, but none came within rifle-shot. At last, at about four in the afternoon, we came to the end of our outward journey. A wall of granite rose before us, with deep caves under it, but offering no possible foothold.

These were the cliffs of Crespo Island, land at last.

Captain Nemo stopped suddenly. This was the end of his kingdom, he did not wish to have anything to do with the land.

We began the return journey. We went back by a different route, which sloped upwards much more steeply.

We came up to a depth of five fathoms, and swarms of little fishes of all sorts darted round us, but we had not yet seen any game worthy of a shot. Then suddenly the captain took aim at some creature moving among the seaweed. He fired, and an animal fell a few yards away.

It was a magnificent sea-otter, the only four-footed beast which lives entirely in the sea. It was about five feet long, and must have been very valuable, with its fine fur, chestnut above, and silver below. The sailor slung it over his shoulder, and we went on. We were walking now on sand, the sea was sometimes so shallow that I could see our reflections on the surface, walking upside-down.

Then a great bird flew low over the sea, and the sailor took aim and fired. It was the prettiest shot I've ever seen. The bird was an albatross, it fell and sank to the feet of the hunter, who picked it up.

We continued our journey, sometimes on sand, sometimes through beds of seaweed, very difficult to cross. I was beginning to be tired, when I saw a faint light. It was the submarine's lamp. I was looking forward to getting on board, for it seemed to me that my air supply was giving out.

I was lagging rather in the rear, when the captain came back, and pushed me to the ground with his strong hand, while the sailor did the same to Counsel. At first I didn't know what to make of this sudden attack, but I saw that the captain was lying down close beside me and keeping quite still. I lay there in the shelter of a clump of weed, when raising my head I saw enormous bodies passing overhead, throwing a phosphorescent light.

The blood froze in my veins. They were sharks, two terrible monsters with huge tails and dull, glassy eyes, with phosphorescent rays coming from holes round their snouts. They could crunch up a whole man in their iron jaws. I shuddered at the sight of their silver bellies and their dreadful mouths bristling with teeth.

Luckily for us, these gluttonous brutes passed without seeing us, though they brushed us with their fins. Our escape was a miracle, for I would rather meet a tiger in the jungle than come face to face with one of these.

Half-an-hour afterwards we reached the *Nautilus*. The outer hatch was still open, and the captain closed it when we were inside. He pressed a button, and the little room was soon pumped dry. We went into the inner room where our diving-suits were taken off and then, stumbling with sleep, I went to my cabin.

16

Four Thousand Leagues Under the Pacific

The next day, November 18th, I was fresh again after a good night's sleep. I went up on deck, at the moment when the first officer was speaking his daily words. It occurred to me then that they meant, 'There is nothing in sight.'

Indeed, the ocean was deserted. Crespo Island had vanished in the night. The sea rippled, a brilliant blue.

I was admiring the water when the captain appeared. He didn't seem to notice me, but started taking bearings. Then he went and leaned on the wheel-house, gazing at the sea.

In the meanwhile, twenty of the crew came up on deck. They started hauling in the nets, which had been out all night. These men seemed to belong to different countries, though they all looked European. I thought I recognised Irishmen, Frenchmen, a few Slavs, and a Greek or Cretan. They did not speak much, and then only in their strange language, so it would have been useless for me to try to talk to them.

The nets were dragged on board, and there was an enormous haul of fish of all sorts. I reckon there must have been almost half a ton. The catch was lowered at once through the hatch on its way to the stores, some to be eaten fresh, the rest to be salted.

I thought the *Nautilus* was going to dive again, and I was making for the hatch, when the captain turned to me, and said,

'You see this ocean, Professor, has it not a life of its own? It has its anger and its gentleness, it has been sleeping, as we have, and now it wakes again after a peaceful night.' He spoke for a long time about the beauty and richness of the sea, which was his only home. Then he went on:

'I could easily imagine towns in the sea, submarine houses, which, like the *Nautilus,* would come up every morning to breathe. They would be free towns, independent cities! And yet, who knows whether some tyrant . . .' He finished his sentence by a violent gesture. Then he went below, and I followed.

During the next few weeks I saw very little of the captain. Counsel and Land spent much of their time with me. Nearly every day the panels in the gallery were opened, and we were never tired of looking at the mysteries of the world under the sea.

The *Nautilus* was moving in a south-easterly direction. On December 1st we crossed the Equator. We saw in the distance the wooded mountains of some of the Pacific islands, but the captain never steered very close to land.

On December 11th, I was reading in the gallery, while Ned and Counsel were watching the lighted waters through the panels. The *Nautilus* was motionless, lying in the deep sea.

'Will the master come here a moment?' said Counsel suddenly in a strange voice.

'What is it, Counsel?' I went over to the window and looked out.

Full in the light from the windows, a huge black mass hung in the water. I watched it closely, trying to make out what sort of whale it was, when another thought struck me:

'A ship!' I cried.

'Yes,' replied the Canadian, 'a sunken wreck.'

The hull of the ship seemed to be in good order, and she could not have been wrecked more than a few hours before. The masts had been cut down close to the deck, in an attempt to save her, but she had heeled over and filled with water.

It was a tragic scene. We stood dumb in our pity. And already I could see great sharks with shining eyes making for the wreck.

Then the *Nautilus* turned round the sunken vessel, and for a moment I could read her name, *Florida, Sunderland*.

17

Stranded in the Torres Straits

After this terrible sight, we saw many other relics of disasters on our voyage. As we were running through busier seas we often saw rotting hulks, and on the ground were cannon, cannon-balls, anchors, chains and other gear eaten by rust. We were passing among the coral islands of the south seas, and we came to the scene of a famous shipwreck which had taken place many years before. The captain showed me the sunken remains of the ships which had perished, and also a tin box, stamped with the royal arms of France, which he had saved from the sea. It contained papers yellow with age, orders from the French Navy for the captain of the expedition, and there were notes in the handwriting of the King of France.

'Ah!' said Captain Nemo, 'it's a fine death for a sailor! A man can lie quiet in a tomb of coral, and I would wish no other for myself and my mates!'

We left those islands and came near to New Guinea. It was January 1st, 1868, and Counsel followed me up on deck.

'May I wish the master a happy New Year?' he said.

'Well, Counsel, that makes me feel as if I were at home, in my study in the Zoo. Thanks for your good wishes! Only, I wish I knew what you mean by a "happy New Year". Shall we escape from our prison this year, or shall we go on with this strange voyage?'

'Indeed, sir,' answered Counsel, 'I really don't know what to say. We certainly haven't been bored, these last two months. Each new wonder is more exciting than the last, and if we go on at this rate, I don't know where we'll end. We shall never have a chance like this again.'

'Never, Counsel.'

'Besides, Captain Nemo is no more trouble to us than if he didn't exist.'

'As you say, Counsel. But what does Ned Land think about it all?'

'Ned Land is exactly the opposite of me. He's tired of always looking at fish and eating them. The lack of wine, bread and meat doesn't suit a good Saxon with a taste for beefsteak, and who's not at all frightened of a drop of gin or brandy!'

'I can't say that I have any complaints about our food.'

'Nor I,' said Counsel. 'I'm quite as anxious to stay on board as Ned is to escape. If this year doesn't turn out well for me, it will for him, and vice versa. So someone will be happy. Anyway, I wish the master whatever will please him best.'

'Thank you, Counsel.'

We passed through the Coral Sea, on the north-east coast of Australia, where Captain Cook was nearly wrecked. Then we drew near to New Guinea, and the captain told me that we were going into the Indian Ocean through Torres Straits, which separate Australia from New Guinea.

These straits bristle with reefs, and the natives in the neighbouring islands are very savage. When we reached the waters of the straits, the captain himself took the wheel, and the *Nautilus* kept to the surface. The water bubbled furiously round the submarine as the currents broke over the coral reefs.

'That's a bad sea!' said Ned.

'Horrible,' I answered, 'and not very suitable for a ship like the *Nautilus*.'

'I hope this confounded captain is certain of his course,' said the Canadian, 'for one of these coral fritters would certainly make a mess of the ship!'

But the submarine seemed to glide by magic among the terrible reefs. However, as we were drawing near to one of the islands, a sudden shock threw me off my feet. The ship had touched a reef, and was stuck fast, with a slight list to port. When I got up, I saw the captain and his first officer on deck, examining the situation. The submarine was undamaged, but she could not move.

The captain, as calm as ever, came over to me.

'An accident?' I asked.

'No, an incident,' he answered.

'But an incident which may force you to become a landsman again!'

The captain gave me a strange look, and shook his head. Then he went on, 'The *Nautilus* is not lost, Mr Aronnax. She will carry you again among the wonders of the ocean. Our voyage is only beginning, and I don't want to lose the pleasure of your company so soon.'

'But, Captain, the tides in these seas are very slight, I don't see how she can float off.'

'It's true that the tides are not very strong, but there's still a difference of a yard and a half between high and low tide. In five days the moon will be full, then I think we shall be refloated.' The captain and the officer went below.

Ned came up to me. 'Well?' he said.

'Well, Ned, we wait patiently for the high tide on the ninth, for it seems that the moon will be kind enough to refloat us.'

'As simple as that? Won't the captain try and haul us off?'

'Why should he, when the tide will do it for us?' said Counsel.

The Canadian shrugged his shoulders. 'Believe me,' he said, 'this hunk of iron will never sail again, either on the sea or below it. It's only good for scrap. I think the moment has come to take our leave of Captain Nemo.'

'Well, Ned,' I replied, 'I don't despair of this brave *Nautilus*. As for escaping, I might agree with you if we were in sight of the British or French coast, but it would be madness here.'

'But can't we have a look at the land, at least?' Ned went on. 'Here is an island, with trees. Under the trees, animals, provided with cutlets and steaks, which I would give a good deal to taste.'

'Ned's right, sir,' said Counsel. 'Couldn't the master get permission from his friend the captain to visit the island, just so that we don't lose the habit of walking on dry land?'

'I can ask him,' I answered, 'but he'll refuse.'

But to my great surprise, Captain Nemo did not refuse. He even gave permission very graciously, without making me promise to return. But to escape into these islands would have been very dangerous.

Next morning, at eight, two of the crew launched the boat for us. We took our seats, armed with electric rifles and axes. The sea was fairly calm, with a slight land breeze. Counsel and I took the oars, while Ned steered through the narrow channels between the reefs. Ned couldn't contain his joy, he felt like an escaped prisoner.

'Meat!' he cried, 'real meat! I don't say that fish isn't a good thing, but you can have too much of it, and I'm looking forward to a piece of fresh venison, grilled over the coals.'

'Pig!' said Counsel. 'You're making my mouth water.'

'It remains to be seen,' I put in, 'first whether there's any game in the forest, and second, whether it's not the sort of game which will hunt the hunters.'

'Well, Mr Aronnax,' said the Canadian, 'I shall certainly eat tiger-steak, if there's nothing else on the island, but whatever happens, any animal with four feet and no feathers, or with two feet and feathers, will be welcome to my gun!'

At half-past eight we beached the boat gently on a sandy shore.

18

Some Days on Land

It was exciting to tread on dry land again, after two months at sea. Ned walked as if he owned the island. We went up the coral beach, towards the mighty forests of the interior. The great trees, some of them two hundred feet tall, were festooned by creepers, with orchids growing among them.

While I was admiring the beauty of the trees, Ned noticed a coconut palm. He knocked down some of the nuts and broke them, and we drank the milk and ate the kernels greedily.

'Excellent!' said Ned.

'Delicious!' said Counsel.

'I don't think your friend the captain would object if we were to carry some on board?' said the Canadian.

'I don't suppose so,' I answered, 'but he wouldn't taste them himself!'

'That's his loss,' said Counsel.

'And our gain!' answered Ned. 'All the more for us!'

'Just a minute, Ned,' I said, as he was starting to attack another tree, 'coconuts are very good things, but before we fill the boat with them, let's see if there isn't anything else on the island. Some fresh vegetables would be welcome.'

'The master is right,' said Counsel, 'and I think we should divide the boat into three parts, one for fruit, one for vegetables, and the third for venison, though I don't see hair nor hide of it.'

'Don't give up hope,' said the Canadian.

'Let's go a little further,' I went on, 'but keeping a good look out. There may be cannibals in these parts.'

'Well,' said Ned, 'I'm beginning to think I could even eat a man myself!'

'Whatever next, Ned?' said Counsel. 'And I share a cabin with you! Shall I wake up one morning to find myself half eaten?'

'Friend Counsel, I'm very fond of you, but not enough to eat you unless I'm driven to it.'

'I don't trust you!' answered Counsel. 'Let's go on with the hunt, we must find some meat for this cannibal!'

We walked on through the forest, and by chance came upon some bread-fruit trees. Ned knew the fruit well, and was dying to taste it.

'Let's have a taste of that bread-fruit,' he said.

'Go ahead,' I answered, 'why not?'

'It won't take long,' said he. With a burning-glass he lit a fire of dead wood which was soon crackling joyfully. In the meantime Counsel and I chose the ripest fruits. They were yellowish and rather soapy and had no stone. Ned cut up a dozen of them into thick slices, and put them to roast on the fire. After a few minutes, he raked out the slices, which were burnt black on the outside, but soft and white inside. They were delicious, tasting rather like artichokes.

'Well, Ned,' I said, 'that was very good. What more do we need?'

'I wouldn't mind some fruit, and perhaps a few vegetables,' he answered.

By midday we had collected a good supply of bananas, some mangoes, and some huge pineapples.

'That's all very fine,' said the harpooner, 'but I want my roast meat.'

'We can try again tomorrow,' said Counsel. 'I think we'd better get back to the boat now.'

We made our way back through the forest, and on the way we found some green vegetables and some little beans. At last, at five o'clock, we loaded the boat with all our loot and made for the submarine. There was no one about. We took the provisions on board, and I went to my cabin. My supper was ready, I ate, and went to bed.

The next day we found the boat lying where we had left it, tied up to the *Nautilus*. It was sunrise, we decided to go ashore again. This time, we let Ned take the lead. We walked along the coast, where there were streams falling into the sea, and climbed into a high plain surrounded by forests. Some kingfishers flew away when we appeared, which made me think that they must have been used to human beings. We came to a little wood, where there were a great many birds.

'Some game at last!' cried Ned.

'Not fit to eat,' said Counsel, 'they're nothing but parrots.'

'I expect parrots are perfectly good to eat,' answered Ned.

The little wood was indeed full of parrots, green, red and blue, flying about and squawking in the branches.

By eleven we had shot nothing, and were very hungry. Then Counsel, to his great surprise, brought down two pigeons at one shot. They were quickly prepared and roasted over a wood fire, and we ate them with bread-fruit. These birds feed on nutmegs, which gives their flesh a most delicious flavour.

'That was good,' I said, 'but I suppose you're not happy yet, Ned?'

'Not till I find a four-legged beast,' he answered.

'Let's go on with the hunt, then,' said Counsel, 'but I think we'd better make for the sea again. We've got to the beginning of the mountains, we ought to have better luck in the forests.'

We turned towards the woods. A few harmless snakes glided away as we drew near, and birds of paradise flew off among the trees. Then by good luck Ned shot a wild pig, to his great delight. After that, Ned and Counsel, beating the thickets, started a troop of small kangaroos. The hunters were wildly excited, and shot down a dozen of them. These little kangaroos make very good eating.

By six o'clock, we were on the beach again, near the boat. The *Nautilus* lay like a great reef two miles offshore. Ned started preparing dinner at once. He was a good cook, and soon a wonderful smell of roast pork perfumed the air.

The dinner was magnificent. As well as the pork chops, we had two pigeons, bread-fruit, some mangoes, and half-a-dozen pineapples, topped off with some fermented coconut milk, which made us very merry.

'Don't let's go back on board tonight!' said Counsel.

'Don't let's ever go back!' said Ned.

At that moment a stone fell at our feet.

19

Captain Nemo's Lightning

We looked towards the forest. A second stone knocked a pigeon's leg out of Counsel's hand. We jumped up, seizing our rifles.

'Is it monkeys?' cried Ned.

'Savages!' said Counsel.

'To the boat!' I cried, making for the sea.

Twenty natives, armed with bows and slings, appeared suddenly on the edge of the wood, not a hundred yards away. They came towards us, showering us with stones and arrows. Ned wouldn't give up his booty, he staggered along with the remains of the pig slung over one shoulder, the kangaroos on the other.

In two minutes we reached the boat, piled the food and guns into it, and shoved off. Soon we were rowing away, while a hundred savages, shouting and waving, dashed up to their waists into the sea. Twenty minutes later, we climbed on board the *Nautilus*. The hatch was open. We moored the boat and went below.

I went into the gallery, where I could hear music. The captain was there, playing on his organ, lost to the world.

'Captain!' I said. He did not hear me.

'Captain!' I repeated, touching his hand,

He shuddered, and turned. 'Oh, it's you, Professor. Well, have you had good hunting?'

'Yes, Captain,' I answered, 'but I'm afraid we've stirred up a troop of two-legged creatures who are rather too close for my liking.'

'What two-legged creatures?'

'Savages.'

'Ah, savages!' said the captain in a sarcastic voice. 'And are you surprised that you meet savages when you set foot on one of the lands of the earth? Are they any worse than other men, these savages of yours?'

'But, Captain . . .'

'Calm yourself, Professor, there's nothing to worry about.'

'But there are a great many of them.'

'How many have you counted?'

'At least a hundred.'

'Mr Aronnax,' said the captain, starting to play again, 'if all the natives of Papua were on the beach the *Nautilus* would have nothing to fear.' He forgot me, lost in his music again.

I went on deck. It was already dark, for in the tropics there is no twilight. I could see many fires lighted on the beach, showing that the natives were not thinking of leaving. But the night passed quietly, and at six next morning I went on deck again. When the mist cleared, I could see the natives, and now there seemed to be about five or six hundred of them. It was low tide, and some of them had climbed out on the coral reefs and were not far from the submarine. I could make them out easily, they were fine figures of men, with woolly hair and black shining bodies. Some of the chiefs wore red and white bead necklaces. They were nearly all armed with bows, arrows, and shields, and carried nets of sling-stones over their shoulders.

While the tide was low, the natives prowled near the *Nautilus*, but they were quite peaceful. They seemed to be inviting me by signs to join them, but I thought it would be wiser not to accept.

So the boat could not go ashore that day, to Ned's great annoyance. He had to content himself with preparing his meat and vegetables, and making a kangaroo pie. The savages went back on shore about eleven, when the rising tide began to cover the coral reefs. As I had nothing better to do, I thought of dragging the clear water with a net, to see if I could find any rare shells. I called Counsel, who brought me a light drag-net, like the ones used for fishing oysters.

'These savages,' said Counsel, 'they don't seem very wicked to me!'

'Yet they're cannibals, you know.'

'I suppose even cannibals can be perfectly decent people,' said he.

We dragged for two hours, without finding anything out of the ordinary. We drew up many shells, a few pearl oysters, and a dozen small turtles which we sent to the galley.

Then I suddenly found something very rare. This was an olive shell in which the spiral turned to the left, instead of to the right, and such a thing is almost unknown in nature. I was enormously excited by this find, and had passed it to Counsel to see, when it was broken in his hand by an unlucky stone slung by one of the natives. Counsel was wild with grief and fury, and seizing my rifle, aimed at the man. I tried to stop him, but he had already fired, and the shot broke the native's bracelet.

'Counsel!' I cried.

'What, sir! The cannibal began it!'

'A shell is not worth a man's life,' I said.

'Ah, the wretch!' said Counsel. 'I would rather he'd broken my arm!' And he meant it too.

We noticed then that the *Nautilus* was surrounded by about twenty pirogues. These native canoes are hollowed out of tree-trunks, balanced by bamboo floats on either side. It was clear that the natives had some knowledge of Europeans, and knew their ships, but they had never seen anything like this long iron tube without a mast or a funnel. They had therefore kept their distance at first, but as the submarine stayed quite still they began to lose their fear. I became alarmed, especially when a shower of arrows came from the pirogues.

'A hailstorm!' said Counsel, 'and maybe the hail is poisoned!'

'I'll warn the captain,' I said, going below.

I went into the gallery. It was empty. I made bold to knock at the door which opened into the captain's cabin.

'Come in,' I heard. I found the captain deep in a mathematical calculation.

'I'm sorry to disturb you, Captain . . .'

'No doubt you have a good reason, Mr Aronnax?'

'Very good, we are surrounded by native pirogues, and in a few minutes we shall certainly be attacked by several hundred savages.'

'Ah,' said the captain calmly, 'they have come with their pirogues?'

'Yes, sir.'

'Well, we have only to close the hatch. Nothing could be easier.' He pressed a button, and gave the order.

'It's done,' he said after a few seconds. 'The boat is in place and the hatch is shut. You don't imagine, I suppose, that these gentle-men can break in the walls which the shells of your frigate could not harm?'

'No, Captain, but tomorrow you will have to open the hatch again, to renew the air . . .'

'Certainly, since we must come up to breathe like the whales.'

'Well, then, the natives will board us the minute the hatch is open!'

'You think they'll come aboard?'

'Certainly they will.'

'Well, let them come. I don't see why we should stop them. They're poor devils, these Papuans, and I don't want my visit here to cost a single one of their lives.' Captain Nemo rose to his feet. 'Tomorrow,' he went on, 'at 2.40 in the afternoon, the *Nautilus* will float undamaged.' He bowed, and I left him and returned to my cabin.

I slept badly that night, for the savages were dancing on deck with ear-splitting yells. But the crew took no more notice of them than soldiers in a fort take of the ants crawling up the walls.

I worked in my cabin next morning, then at half-past two I went into the gallery. In ten minutes, according to the captain's promise, the submarine should be free of the reef. If not, she would have to stay there for many months.

However, I felt a trembling in the hull of the ship, and heard the grating of the steel on the reef.

At two-thirty-five Captain Nemo came into the gallery.

'We're off,' he said. 'I've given the order to open the hatch.'

'And the Papuans? Won't they climb on board?'

'Mr Aronnax,' the captain answered calmly, 'one does not climb into the *Nautilus* just like that, even when the hatch is open. You don't understand?'

'Not at all.'

'Come with me, then, and you'll see.' I went to the central ladder. Ned and Counsel were watching several of the crew opening the hatch, while cries of rage and horrible screams came from outside. As soon as it was open, twenty fierce warriors sprang up. But the first to put his hand on the rail of the ladder shot backwards, and disappeared waving his arms and shrieking. Ten of his fellows suffered the same fate.

Counsel was wild with joy. Ned rushed to the ladder, but as soon as he put his hands on the rail, he also was thrown back.

'The devil!' he cried, 'I've been struck by lightning!'

These words explained everything. The hand-rail was charged with electricity, not enough to kill, but only to give a sharp shock. The Papuans had fled, mad with terror. We laughed at poor Ned as we consoled him and rubbed him, while he swore like one possessed.

At that moment the tide reached the full, and the *Nautilus* left her coral bed exactly at that fortieth minute fixed by the captain. The screw beat the water, then the speed increased and she came safe and sound out of the dangerous channels of Torres Straits.

20

Drugged

We were voyaging now many miles from land, and it became difficult to imagine any other life, when something happened which reminded us of the strangeness of our situation.

On January 18th, the *Nautilus* was several hundred miles from the nearest coast. The sky was overcast, the sea choppy under the east wind. The barometer had been falling for some days and a storm threatened.

I came up on deck just as the first officer was taking his daily bearings, and I listened for the usual phrase. But that day the words were different. Almost at once the captain appeared, and started scanning the horizon with his glass.

For a few minutes he stared fixedly at a certain point, then he lowered his glass and talked with the officer. The captain was calm, as usual, but the other seemed hardly able to control his excitement. I stared at the sea, but could make out nothing at all.

The captain meanwhile was pacing the deck. Sometimes he stopped and gazed at the sea with his arms folded. The officer was looking through the telescope again, walking to and fro in nervous excitement. Then he called to the captain and pointed something out to him. This was too much for me, I went down to the gallery to fetch a telescope. But no sooner had I got it to my eye than it was snatched from my grasp.

I turned round. Captain Nemo was in front of me, but I hardly recognised him. His face was changed, his eyes gleamed fiercely under knitted brows, his teeth were bared. He stood stiffly, with clenched fists, his head sunk between his shoulders, his whole body charged with hatred. He did not move. My glass, fallen from his hand, had rolled to his feet.

I wondered what I could have done to rouse his fury, then I realised that it was not directed against me. His eye remained fixed on that distant point of the horizon.

At last he came to himself. He spoke a few words to his officer, then turned to me.

'Mr Aronnax,' he said in an imperious tone, 'I must ask you to fulfil the condition you undertook.'

'What do you mean, Captain?'

'You and your companions must be shut up until I see fit to release you.'

'You are the master,' I answered. 'But may I ask you one question?'

'None, sir.'

There was nothing to be said. I went down to Ned and Counsel and told them. Ned was furious, of course, but there was no time to argue. Four men waited at the door, and took us to the cell where we had spent our first night on board. Ned's protests were cut short by the slamming of the door.

'Can the master tell us what it's all about?' said Counsel.

I told them what had happened, then started turning it all over in my mind, but without making any sense of it. Then Ned exclaimed,

'Well, anyway, lunch is ready.' I looked at the table. 'They've sent us nothing but the ship's rations,' he went on.

'Better than nothing!' said Counsel.

We ate in silence. I took very little, Counsel made himself eat, as a 'wise precaution', but nothing could upset Ned's appetite. After lunch we made ourselves as comfortable as we could on the floor.

At that moment, the electric light went out and left us in complete darkness. Ned fell asleep at once, and to my surprise, Counsel also dropped off very soon. I was wondering what had made him so sleepy, when I found that I too had difficulty in keeping my eyes open. Our food must have been drugged, the captain did not think it enough to shut us up! I heard the hatch close. The ship did not roll now, as she had done before, and I wondered if she had dived. Then the drug overpowered me, and I sank into a heavy sleep.

21

Death of a Seaman

The next day, I woke with a surprisingly clear head. To my astonishment I was in my cabin. I tried the door, and found it unlocked. I was quite free. I found the hatch open, and went on deck.

Ned and Counsel were there. They too had woken up in their cabin, and knew no more than I. The *Nautilus* seemed quiet and mysterious as before, moving at a steady speed on the surface. Nothing was changed.

Ned scanned the horizon with his long-sighted eyes, but he could see nothing, neither sail nor shore. The wind blew from the west, ruffling the long waves and making the ship roll. The *Nautilus*, after renewing her air, kept to a depth of fifty feet, so that she could surface again quickly. This she did several times that day, against her usual practice, and the first officer came up on deck and spoke his accustomed words.

The captain did not appear. I saw only the steward, who served me as well and as silently as ever.

About two o'clock I was writing in the gallery when the captain came in. I wished him good-day, he nodded slightly without speaking. I went on with my work, hoping he would tell me something of what had happened the night before. But he said nothing. He looked tired, his eyes were red as if he had not slept, and there was a look of deep sorrow on his face. He wandered about the room, sat down and got up again, took up a book and laid it down, consulted his instruments without taking the usual notes, and did not seem able to keep still. At last he came to me and said,

'Are you a doctor, Mr Aronnax?' I was so surprised by this question that I stared at him for some time without answering.

'Are you a doctor?' he repeated. 'Several of your colleagues have taken medical degrees, I know.'

'Yes,' I said, 'certainly I'm a doctor. I practised for several years before going to the Museum.'

'Good. Will you see one of my men?'

'You have a sick man?'

'Yes.'

'I'll come at once.' I followed him in great excitement. Perhaps I should learn something of what had happened. The captain led me aft, into a cabin near the crew's quarters. There lay the sick man, who looked like an Englishman. His head was bound in bloodstained bandages. I removed the dressings, while he looked at me with great staring eyes, uttering no sound.

It was a horrible wound. The skull had been split by a blunt instrument, laying bare the brain. The man's breathing was slow, his face twitched spasmodically, his feet and legs were already growing cold. Death was not far off. There was nothing to be done for him, but I dressed the wound, then turned to the captain.

'What was the cause of this wound?' I asked.

'What does it matter! A sudden shock broke a lever of one of the motors. There were two men there, this one threw himself in front of the other, and took the full force of the blow. A man laid down his life for his friend, that's all. What do you think of his condition?' I hesitated. 'You can speak out,' he went on. 'He doesn't understand French.'

'He will be dead in two hours.'

'Nothing can save him?'

'Nothing.'

The captain's hand clenched convulsively, a few tears started from his eyes, which were not made for weeping.

For a little time I watched the dying man, from whose face the colour was slowing ebbing under the bright light. It was an intelligent face, with deep lines of sorrow and misfortune.

I slept badly that night, and my dreams were interrupted by distant singing, a dirge for the seaman who had died.

His comrades buried him next morning in a coral cemetery deep under the waves. There they dug his grave beside graves of others of their number, in the bed of the sea, to be covered by the coral which grew all round that place. I went with them, and when we were back on board, and had changed out of our diving-suits, I spoke to the captain.

'So you have buried your friend in the coral cemetery?'

'Yes, forgotten by the world, but not by us. We dig the grave, and the polyps seal the tomb for eternity.' He hid his face in his hands, then went on, 'That is our quiet graveyard, a hundred feet under the surface of the waves!'

'Your dead sleep in peace, Captain, out of the reach of sharks!'

'Yes,' he answered gravely, 'of sharks and men.'

22

The Pearl-Diver and the Shark

At four o'clock next morning I was called by the steward. I was to take part in a trip to the pearl fisheries which the captain had proposed. I dressed quickly and found the captain in the gallery.

'Are you ready, Mr Aronnax?'

'Yes, I'm ready. Should we put on our diving-suits?'

'Not yet. I didn't want to bring the ship too far in, so we'll take the boat, then we shan't have such a long journey on foot.'

We found Ned and Counsel on deck, in great excitement about the trip. The boat was manned by the coxswain and four rowers. We three with Captain Nemo sat aft, the moorings were slipped and we made towards the land. It was still dark, the sky was overcast, and I could make out nothing of the land but an uneven line on the horizon. The rowers made long, steady strokes, there was a slight swell.

The day broke suddenly, about six o'clock, and I could see land clearly, with a few trees here and there. At a sign from the captain the anchor was dropped, and the chain hardly ran out at all, since the bottom was scarcely a yard deep.

'Here we are, then,' said the captain. 'The pearl-fishing boats anchor in that bay over there. Now we'll get into our diving-gear.' We four put on our suits with the help of the seamen, who were not coming with us. Before getting into my helmet, I asked the captain whether we should need the flash lamps.

'They wouldn't be of any use,' he said. 'We shan't go deep, and the daylight will be enough. In any case, it's not very wise to show bright lights in these waters, we might attract some nasty customers.'

I looked at Ned and Counsel, but they had put on their helmets and were deaf and dumb, for all practical purposes.

'What about our guns, Captain?'

'Guns! What's the use? Your mountaineers take knives when they go after bears, and isn't steel surer than lead? Here's a good blade, stick it in your belt and we'll be off.'

Ned and Counsel were armed likewise, and Ned had taken a great harpoon as well. So I put on my helmet and we were all ready. The sailors helped us into the sea, one by one. We walked downhill and soon were under the surface. I found that my panic had left me, and I was very much interested in all I saw. We were in about fifteen feet of water, and could see quite clearly. There were all sorts of fascinating sea-creatures, including a giant crab, the sort that can climb coconut trees, shake down the nuts, and extract the kernels with its mighty claws. Here under the water it scuttled away with great speed.

About seven o'clock we came at last to the oyster-bed. Millions of oysters clung to the rocks, attached by brown tissues and unable to move. The shells are round and very rough outside, some of them were about six inches across. The captain pointed out this inexhaustible mine, while Ned fell on the spoils and filled his net with shells.

But we were not allowed to linger. The captain led us on by paths known to him alone, between rocky pinnacles, where monstrous crayfish lurked in crevices, looking at us with staring eyes, till we came to a huge cave. He led the way through the rocky entrance. It seemed very dark inside at first, but after a few moments I could make out great natural pillars holding up the vaulted roof. We walked down a steep slope, and found ourselves in the bottom of a sort of well. There the captain stopped and pointed.

I saw an enormous oyster, over six feet across, larger than the shell in the gallery of the *Nautilus*. It was growing on a granite slab, developing alone in the calm waters of the cave. The captain evidently knew about this oyster, and had visited it before. The valves were half open, and he bent down and fixed his dagger between the shells to prevent them from closing, then with his hand he raised the fringed beard. There, resting between the folds of flesh, I saw a pearl the size of a coconut. It was exquisite in form and colour, a jewel of inestimable price. In my excitement I stretched out my hand to touch and weigh it, but the captain stopped me, drew out his knife and let the two valves close.

He left it there to grow year after year, and one day he would take it for his collection. It was certainly a museum piece rather than a jewel, for no woman could have worn it.

We came away from the grotto, and wandered over the oyster-bed. I had completely forgotten the possibility of danger. For a time I was walking with my head above the surface. Counsel came up to me, and sticking his great swelled head close to mine, he winked at me through the glass. Then the ground sloped away again, and we were back in our element – as the sea had now become for us. Suddenly the captain stopped, and signed to us to lie doggo close to him under a jutting rock. He pointed at something dark moving in the water. Sharks! I thought, but I was wrong, for it was a man, a Cingalese diver.

I could see the bottom of his canoe a few feet above his head. I saw, too, the stone between his feet and the line linking him to the boat. When he was down he knelt and filled his net hastily with oysters pulled up at random, then he bobbed back to the surface, and a few minutes later dived again.

He could not see us, for we were hidden in the shadow of the rock. Suddenly he started with horror and sprang up. A shadow appeared above the wretched man, it was a huge shark bearing down with gleaming eyes and open jaws. I was rooted to the ground with terror. The brute swept down, the Cingalese managed to throw himself clear of the snapping teeth, but he did not avoid the tail, which knocked him flat on the ground. All this took only a few seconds. The shark turned on its back and was about to cut the man in two, when Captain Nemo sprang up and went for the monster, knife in hand. The shark, seeing this new enemy, turned towards him. The captain waited, and when the great fish attacked him he stepped nimbly aside and thrust the dagger into its belly. But that was not the end.

Blood rushed from the wound, staining the sea red, so that I could see nothing. Then the water cleared and I caught a glimpse of the captain, hanging on to one of the shark's fins and with repeated knife-thrusts trying to find the creature's heart. The frenzied brute lashed the water with its tail and I was almost thrown over by the eddies. I wanted to help, but I was still paralysed by horror and could not move. The captain fell to the ground, overthrown by the huge weight of the shark, which opened its jaws like a pair of monstrous shears. That would have been the end of him, but Ned Land rushed forward, quick as lightning, and thrust his harpoon deep into the monster's side. The sea was a mass of blood, beaten into boiling surge by the death-throes of the shark, for Ned had driven home.

The captain got up unharmed, went at once to the Cingalese,

cut the cord which tied the stone to his feet, and taking him in his arms, swam with him to the surface. We all followed, and climbed into the diver's boat.

The captain was trying to revive the Cingalese. He had not been under water for long, but the blow from the shark's tail might have killed him. Vigorous rubbing soon brought him back to life, however, and he opened his eyes. The poor man must have been terrified at the sight of the four great copper heads leaning over him. Then the captain drew from his pocket a little bag of pearls, and put it into the diver's hand. He took it in fear and trembling, thinking no doubt that we were creatures from another world.

Then we returned to our boat, and the sailors helped us out of our diving-kit. The captain's first word was for the Canadian.

'Thank you, Ned,' he said.

'Tit for tat,' said Ned. 'I owed you that.'

The captain smiled slightly. 'To the *Nautilus*,' he said.

The boat shot over the waves. A few minutes later, we came up against the floating corpse of the shark. I saw then that it was about twenty-five feet long, with a mouth a third the length of its body. While I watched it, a dozen living sharks appeared all round the boat, but they were not interested in us, for they threw themselves on the body and started tearing it to pieces.

When we got back on board, I found myself wondering why the captain, who had cut himself off from the human race, should have risked his life to save the Cingalese. When I spoke of this to him, he answered,

'That man comes from a downtrodden race, and while I live such men are my brothers.'

23

The Red Sea

During January 29th, Ceylon sank below the horizon, and we were set on a course north-north-west through the maze of islands. We had travelled sixteen thousand two hundred and twenty miles, or seven thousand five hundred leagues since our starting point in the seas of Japan. We were heading for the Gulf of Oman, which leads into the Persian Gulf, from which there is no other outlet. I wondered where we were going, and though for my part I was happy to leave our course to the captain, this would not do for Ned.

'If we go up the Persian Gulf,' he said, 'we'll only have to come out again.'

'Then we could visit the Red Sea,' I answered.

'Another dead end, since the Suez Canal is not cut yet, and even if it were, a mysterious ship like ours would never venture into its locks. We shan't get to Europe that way.'

'Perhaps by the Cape of Good Hope?'

'Do you realise, Professor, that we've been prisoners for three months?'

'I must say, Ned, I don't feel like a prisoner. But if you can ever come to me and say, "Now's our chance to escape", I'll talk to you then.'

We entered the Gulf of Oman, and stayed there aimlessly for a few days, then on February 5th we went on, and came to Aden. I thought we should turn back, but we continued through the Straits of Bab-el-Mandeb, which lead into the Red Sea. We kept dived during the passage of the Straits, since the captain did not want to run into any English or French steamers on the lines from Suez to India, Australia, or the French possessions in the Far East.

We made our way up the Red Sea, and there were plenty of new and exciting submarine wonders to be seen through the glass panels of the gallery. Particularly I noticed sponges of all shapes and sizes.

On February 9th I was on deck, when the captain appeared. I made up my mind to find out where we were going next. He came up to me, and offered me a cigar.

'Well, Professor, how do you like the Red Sea? Plenty to interest a naturalist, I think.'

'Certainly, Captain, and the *Nautilus* makes a splendid observation post. She's an intelligent ship.'

'Indeed she is, intelligent, brave, and invulnerable! She has no need to fear the terrible storms of the Red Sea, nor its currents, nor its reefs.'

'Your ship is at least a hundred years before her time, Captain, it's a pity that such a secret must die with its inventor!' The captain made no answer. Then he said, rather stiffly,

'The Red Sea is so called because of the colour of its waters.'

'All the same, it looks just like any other water to me.'

'You get the colour towards the head of the gulf. Up there, I've seen it all red, like a lake of blood.'

'And the colour comes from microscopic algae, or sea-plants,

I believe. So this isn't the first time you've navigated these waters?'

'No.'

'Then tell me, have you found any traces of Pharaoh's chariot wheels?'

'No, and for a very good reason. The place where Moses crossed over with all his people is now so silted up with sand that camels can hardly get their legs wet, so you see the water is too shallow for the ship's draught.'

'A pity. And I suppose that even if the Suez Canal were finished, you would hardly want to risk the passage with your precious *Nautilus*?'

'I wonder.' He smiled. 'But even if I can't take you through the canal yet, you'll be able to see the long moles of Port Said the day after tomorrow, when we shall be in the Mediterranean.'

'In the Mediterranean!' I cried.

'That surprises you?'

'The *Nautilus* will have to go like the wind, to get round the Cape of Good Hope and into the Mediterranean by the day after tomorrow!'

'Who said anything about the Capc of Good Hope?'

'Well, the *Nautilus* can hardly sail on dry land over the isthmus . . .'

'What about underneath the isthmus?'

'Whatever do you mean?'

He smiled again. 'There's a subterranean passage, which I have named the Arabian Tunnel. It opens below Suez and comes out near Port Said.'

'Good heavens! Did you discover it by chance?'

'Rather by common sense.'

'Would it be tactless to ask you how you found it?'

'There's no need for secrecy between men who are bound

together for life. I found it by watching the fishes, and I'm the only man who knows it. I noticed that there are a certain number of fish of exactly the same kinds in both the Mediterranean and the Red Sea, and that set me thinking. If there were such a passage, it would have to run from the Red Sea northward, as the level is higher in the Red Sea. So I caught a great number of fish in the neighbourhood of Suez, ringed them round the tail with copper rings, and threw them back into the sea. Several months later, off Syria, I caught some of my ringed fish, and proved my point. Then I looked for the tunnel with my *Nautilus*, found it, and risked the voyage. Soon you'll know it too!'

24

The Arabian Tunnel

I told Ned and Counsel about the tunnel, and Counsel was delighted, while Ned remained most doubtful. I was sitting with them on deck on February 10th, the sea was deserted, and we talked of this and that while we watched the misty Arabian coast.

Suddenly Ned pointed towards the sea, saying, 'Do you see something there?'

'No, Ned, but I haven't got your eyes.'

'There, starboard ahead! There's something moving – some sea-beast.' I could make out a long black body on the surface.

'Are there whales in the Red Sea?' said Counsel.

'Yes, indeed there are,' cried Ned, 'but it's not a whale, trust me for that.'

We were closer now to the creature, and I realised what it was. 'It's a dugong,' I cried. 'A sort of sea-cow. They're getting very rare.'

Ned's eyes gleamed. He was dying to get at it with his harpoon. 'Gosh!' he said. 'I've never killed one of those!'

Then the captain came up on deck. He saw the dugong, and knew at once how Ned was feeling.

'Well, Ned, you're itching for your harpoon, aren't you?'

'You've said it, Captain.'

'Go ahead, then.' Ned was overjoyed. 'Only, I warn you, don't miss it. It's quite capable of turning on you and smashing the boat to bits. But you're too old a hand to need a warning. Bring it in, and I'll promise you a good dinner.'

'They're good to eat too?' said the harpooner.

'Indeed they are, in Malay they are kept for royal banquets. In fact, they're hunted so eagerly that they're getting rare.'

'Shouldn't we preserve it, then, in the interests of science?' said Counsel.

'Let him have his sport,' said the captain. At that moment, seven of the crew, silent and calm as usual, came up on deck. One carried a harpoon and line. The boat was launched, the coxswain and the rowers took their places. Ned, Counsel and I sat aft.

The captain wished us 'Good hunting!' and we rowed towards the dugong, which lay sleeping on the water about two miles away. When we were a few cables from it, our speed slackened and we came on quietly. Ned went to the bows, harpoon in hand. The line was fastened to a small barrel which would float and show where the animal went. It was a huge creature, about twenty feet long. The rowers rested on their oars, while Ned aimed his weapon. Suddenly there was a whistling noise and the sea-cow disappeared. It looked as if the harpoon had only struck the water.

'The devil!' cried the Canadian in fury. 'Missed!'

'It's wounded,' I said, 'see the blood. But the harpoon hasn't stuck.'

'My harpoon!' cried Ned. The men bent to their oars, the coxswain steering towards the floating barrel. When we had fished up the harpoon, we set off in pursuit of the dugong. From time to time it surfaced to breathe, and the wound must only have been slight, for its pace was terrific. Ned was raging mad, and swore horribly at the creature in English.

The chase lasted for an hour, and I thought the quarry was going to get away, when it suddenly turned and started to attack us.

'Look out!' cried Ned. The coxswain spoke to the men, no doubt warning them. The dugong stopped short twenty feet from the boat, sniffed the air, then hurled itself on us. We rocked violently and shipped a lot of water, but thanks to skilful handling we were not upset. Ned, clinging on with one hand, struck again and again with his harpoon. The beast had gripped the gunwale in its teeth and was hoisting the boat out of the water like a lion savaging a goat. We were all piled on top of one another, clinging on for dear life, but at last Ned managed to strike the animal to the heart.

I heard its teeth grating on the armour-plating, and it sank, dragging the harpoon with it. But soon the barrel bobbed up again, and a few minutes later the body appeared, floating on its back. The boat went after it and took it in tow, then we made for the submarine. They had to use powerful tackle to hoist the dugong on deck, it weighed five tons. The same day I ate several slices of the meat, which tasted very good, rather like beef.

The next day we caught some sea-swallows and about a dozen Nile ducks, which are also very good to eat.

We were nearing the head of the Red Sea, and in the distance I caught a glimpse of Mount Sinai. When we were off Tor, at six o'clock, I noticed the red colour in the water. Then night fell in a heavy silence, broken at times by the cry of a pelican or some night-bird, the sound of surf on the rocks or the distant beating of a paddle-steamer.

From eight to nine we were submerged, then we surfaced and

I went up on deck. I was excited by the thought of the tunnel, and I wanted a breath of fresh air. Soon I saw a faint light about a mile away.

'It's the Suez lightship,' said the captain's voice, close beside me. 'We'll soon reach the tunnel now.'

'It must be rather tricky, finding the entrance?'

'It is. I always take the wheel myself. Now we must go below, we're going to dive, and we'll surface in the Mediterranean.'

I went down after him. The hatch was shut, the tanks filled, and we dived to thirty feet. I was turning towards my cabin when the captain stopped me.

'Would you like to come into the wheel-house with me?'

I was as excited as a schoolboy. We went to the central ladder. Half-way up, he opened a door, and we went forward along the upper passage-way till we came to the wheel-house. It was about six feet square, rather like those on the Mississippi or Hudson River steamboats. The wheel was in the centre, and there were four portholes, one in each wall. It was dark inside, but soon I made out the helmsman, leaning over the wheel. Outside the sea was lit up by the lamp in its tower aft.

'Now,' said the captain, 'we must look for the tunnel's mouth.' His orders were passed by electric signals to the motor-room. He pressed a switch, and our speed slackened considerably.

I looked out at the sheer rock wall close beside us, while the captain kept his eyes on the compass, directing the helmsman.

At ten-fifteen the captain took the wheel. A great black cavern opened before us, and the *Nautilus* plunged in. There was a rushing noise as the waters hurried down the slope of the tunnel. The *Nautilus* sped like an arrow down the stream, though the motors were running hard astern to counteract the rush as much as possible.

The narrow rock walls were streaked and lined with light as

the ship dashed by, my heart was beating violently.

At ten-thirty-five the captain handed over the wheel to the helmsman and turned to me. 'The Mediterranean,' he said.

In less than twenty minutes the *Nautilus* had passed under the isthmus of Suez.

25

The Isles of Greece

The next day, February 12th, the *Nautilus* surfaced at dawn. I rushed up on deck. Three miles to southward I saw the vague outline of Port Said. About seven, Ned and Counsel came and joined me, after a quiet night's sleep.

'Well, what about this Mediterranean?' said the Canadian in a grumpy voice.

'This is it,' I said.

'What!' said Counsel, 'last night . . .'

'Last night, as ever was, we crossed the uncrossable isthmus in several minutes.'

'Don't believe a word of it,' said Ned.

'Stubborn as a mule,' I said. 'Look south, there's the Egyptian coast.'

'So you say.'

'Anyway, Ned, I was with the captain in the wheel-house while we went through the tunnel.'

'Listen to that, Ned,' said Counsel.

'Use your eyes, old chap, you can see the piers of Port Said running out into the sea.' Ned looked.

'Well, I'll be blowed,' he said at last, 'so they are. I take off my hat to the captain. Now, that's all very fine, at last we can get down to business. There's no one about.'

I knew what was biting him, and thought it best to let him get it off his chest. So we went and sat near the lamp, where there was less spray.

'Now, Ned, let's have it.'

'Only this,' he said. 'We're in Europe, and before the captain takes it into his head to drag us off to the North Pole or back to the China seas, let's get the hell out of here.'

I hated this talk. I was very happy on board, the strange character of the captain intrigued me and I was re-writing my book on the 'Mysteries of the Sea' in the very heart of my subject. On the other hand, I had a duty to my mates.

'Tell me frankly, Ned, are you sorry that we ever came?'

He thought for a minute, then answered, 'Frankly, then, no, I'm not sorry. I'm glad we've made this underwater trip, but I shall be very glad when it's over. That's my feeling.'

'One day it will be over.'

'Yes, but when and where?'

'The captain is sure to let us go,' said Counsel, 'when we've visited all the oceans of the world.'

'I don't agree,' I said. 'He'll never let us go, we know too much.'

'What are you waiting for, then?' said the Canadian.

Indeed, I only wanted to delay our escape for six months or so, till I had seen all I wanted to see, but Ned was not to be put off. Counsel was no help, he refused to take sides in the argument. At last I had to give in.

'All right, Ned,' I said. 'I agree with you that we ought to take the first opportunity to escape. There's only one thing, we must be quite sure that the first attempt comes off. If it fails and we've given ourselves away, we'll never get a second chance, and the captain will never forgive us.'

'Agreed,' said Ned. 'The first dark night, then, when the ship is near enough to the coasts of Europe.'

'You're planning to swim?'

'If we're near enough, and surfaced. If not, we'll take the boat. I know how it works. The helmsman looks the other way, we'd be safe enough.'

'All right, Ned, it's up to you. Let us know and we'll be with you.' I thought, however, that the captain would take special precautions to give us no chance to escape in these busy seas, and it seemed that I was right. The *Nautilus* kept submerged as much as possible, and stayed well away from land. When she surfaced, it was only to the level of the wheel-house.

On February 14th I wanted to watch the fish, but the shutters remained firmly closed. In disgust I went to look at the chart, and saw that we were approaching Crete. At the time I sailed from America on the *Abraham Lincoln*, the people of the island had just risen in revolt against their Turkish overlords, but I had no idea whether the rising had been successful or not. Certainly the captain would know nothing, since he had no communication with the world.

I found myself alone with him in the gallery that evening, but he was silent and moody, and I thought it better not to question him about the Cretan rising. Then he had the shutters opened, and paced from one window to another, watching the water. I spent my time taking notes of the many strange fishes.

Suddenly a diver appeared in the water. He swam vigorously, sometimes surfacing to breathe, then diving again. I turned to the captain, who was at the other window.

'A man!' I cried, 'a shipwrecked sailor! Can't we save him?'

The captain said nothing, but came to the window. The man

came close and looked through the glass. To my utter astonishment the captain made him a sign. The diver waved in reply, then swam upwards and did not reappear.

'Don't worry,' said the captain. 'It's Nicholas, of Cape Matapan, called the Fish. He's well known throughout the Cyclades. A bold diver! He lives in the water, and knows all the islands from here to Crete.'

'You know him, then?'

'Why not?' The captain went to a safe standing by the port window of the gallery. On the floor near by I saw an ironbound case, with a brass plate on its lid bearing the ship's name. He opened the safe, and I saw that it was filled with gold bars. My eyes were popping out of my head as the captain, taking no notice of me, began to pack the case with the gold bars, stowing them carefully till the box was full.

He padlocked the case, and wrote on the lid an address in modern Greek characters. Then he pressed a button, four men appeared, and with much difficulty pushed the case out of the gallery. Then I heard them raising it up the iron ladder with hoisting tackle. The captain turned to me,

'You were saying, Professor?'

'I said nothing, Captain.'

'Allow me, then, to wish you a very good night.' He left the room.

I went to my cabin, my head reeling with wild guesses. Surely there must be some connection between the appearance of the diver and the case of gold. Soon I felt that the ship was surfacing, then I heard steps on deck. The boat was being launched, I heard it bumping against the ship's side, then there was silence.

After two hours I heard the boat come back. More footsteps overhead, the sound of the boat being screwed down, and the *Nautilus* dived. So the gold had been delivered to its address.

The next day I told Ned and Counsel about the strange happenings of the night.

'But where the devil does he get all those millions?' said Ned.

On February 16th we came out of the deep basin between Rhodes and Alexandria, passed round Cape Matapan, and left the Greek Islands behind us.

26

Through the Mediterranean

We passed through the blue waters of the Mediterranean in forty-eight hours, so that I could see very little of that famous sea, with its orange groves, cactus and pines, and the rugged mountains on its shores. The captain himself did not appear once during those two days, and it seemed to me that the waters of that sea must be too full of memories and sorrows for him to linger there.

Our speed was twenty-one knots, so poor Ned had to give up his escape plan. He could hardly hope to use the boat at that speed; it would have been like jumping off a moving train. Besides this, we remained submerged except at night, when we surfaced to renew the air, and we navigated by instruments.

Counsel and I had to content ourselves with watching what fish we could, since we saw nothing of the land. We saw lampreys, sturgeons, tunny-fish, and many others, and among the sea mammals there were two or three sperm whales, some dolphins, and a dozen seals.

We had to pass slowly over the great submarine barrier which stretches between Sicily and the coast of Tunis, where the continents of Europe and Africa were once joined. When we were over this bar, the *Nautilus* put on speed again, and dived right to the bottom of this deep stretch of sea.

There was little submarine life there, but many wrecks. As we drew near to the Straits of Gibraltar the number of rotting hulks lying on the sea-bed increased, as these narrow waters have always been dangerous to shipping. But the *Nautilus* ran at great speed past these ruins. On February 18th, about three in the morning, we arrived at the Straits.

The submarine dived deep and sped through. I had a brief glimpse of the ruins of the ancient temple of Hercules, now sunken beneath the sea, then we were in the Atlantic Ocean.

27

Vigo Bay

When the submarine had passed through the Straits of Gibraltar, she made for the open sea. Then she rode on the surface, and we were able to take our daily strolls in the fresh air again.

I was on deck with Ned and Counsel. We saw the vague outline of Cape St Vincent a dozen miles away, there was a fairly strong south wind, the sea had a heavy swell. There was too much water breaking over the deck to be comfortable, so we went down again after a few mouthfuls of ozone. I went to my cabin, Counsel disappeared, but Ned followed me in.

When the door was shut, he sat down and looked at me in silence.

'I know what you feel, Ned, but it wasn't any good, we couldn't leave the ship at that speed!' He said nothing, sitting there with tight lips and a frown on his brow. 'Don't take it to heart,' I went on. 'We're following the Portuguese coast. France and England lie beyond, where we shall easily find a refuge. We're keeping in civilised waters, the chance is sure to come.'

He still stared at me, then at last he spoke.

'It's for tonight,' he said. I was overcome, I didn't know what to say. 'We'd agreed to wait for a chance,' he went on. 'This is our chance. This evening we shall be only a few miles from the Spanish coast. It will be dark. The wind's blowing on shore. You gave me your word.'

I still said nothing. He got up and came to lean over me.

'Tonight at nine o'clock. I've warned Counsel. The captain will be in his cabin, probably in bed. None of the crew will be able to see us. Counsel and I will go to the central ladder. You stay in the library and wait for my signal. The oars, mast and sail are in the boat, and I've even managed to stow some rations. I have a spanner to unscrew the boat. Till this evening, then.'

'It's a rough sea,' I said.

'We've got to take some risk, it's worth it. It's a good boat. Tomorrow we may be a hundred miles out. If we get any luck, we'll be ashore by ten or eleven, otherwise, we'll be in Davy Jones's locker. See you tonight!' He went out, leaving me in a turmoil. It was terribly sudden, no time to think or discuss. But Ned was right, we might never get so good a chance again.

At that moment there was a loud whistling as the tanks filled up, and the *Nautilus* dived. I stayed in my cabin, I wanted to avoid the captain, feeling that I could not meet his eyes.

I spent a miserable day, torn between the need to get away while the going was good and my desire to go on with the voyage, to study the submarine life of the Atlantic and so complete my knowledge. Several times I went to the gallery, to look at the compass. The *Nautilus* was still keeping to Portuguese waters, heading north. As for luggage, I had only my notes. I had not seen the captain for some days, and I wondered whether in fact he did stay on board all the time. I knew now that he had still some friends on land.

The day dragged out, minute by minute, but at last my dinner was brought to me, though I had little appetite. I left the table at seven – in two hours I must join Ned. I couldn't keep still, but paced up and down in a fever, my heart beating wildly.

I decided to make one last visit to the gallery. I had spent so many happy hours there, among its strange and beautiful treasures. As I wandered round the room, I found to my surprise that the door leading to the captain's cabin was ajar. I drew back, but there was no sound, so I cautiously pushed the door open. The cabin was empty, I stepped inside. The room still looked bare and severe, like a monk's cell, but I saw some engravings hanging on the wall which I had not noticed on my last visit. They were the portraits of great men of history whose lives had been spent in the service of their fellow-men: Kosciusko, the Polish hero; Daniel O'Connell, defender of Ireland; George Washington, founder of the United States; Abraham Lincoln, killed by the slave-owner's bullet; and lastly John Brown, martyr to the cause of Negro freedom, hanging on his gallows. Were these portraits the clue to Captain Nemo's mystery? Was he the champion of oppressed peoples, the liberator of enslaved races? I thought he must have played some part in recent underground movements, or perhaps he was a hero of the American Civil War.

The clock struck eight. I looked at the compass, we were still heading north, the log showed a moderate speed, the depth-gauge read sixty feet. Everything was in favour of Ned's plan.

I went back to my cabin and dressed myself warmly; sea-boots, otter-fur cap, tunic of seaweed fibre lined with sealskin. I was ready. Only the regular beat of the screw disturbed the silence. I listened in an agony of suspense – perhaps Ned would be found out. At a few minutes to nine, I listened at the captain's door. No sound. I left my cabin and went back to the gallery, which was dimly lighted and empty. I opened the door to the library. No one there. I went to stand by the door which opened on the well of the central ladder, to wait for Ned's signal.

At that moment, the screw-beats slackened, then stopped. What was the matter? I could near nothing but the beating of my heart. Then came a slight bump as the *Nautilus* settled on the floor of the ocean. No signal from Ned. In sudden panic I thought of trying to find him, to get him to put off the escape.

At that moment the door from the gallery opened, and the captain came in.

'Ah, Professor,' he said in a friendly tone, 'I was looking for you. Do you know the history of Spain?'

I was struck dumb. If I had been asked my own name at that moment, I couldn't have answered.

'Well,' he went on, 'do you know the history of Spain?'

I pulled myself together. 'Not very well,' I stammered.

'Ah!' said he, 'the ignorance of the learned! Come and sit down, and I'll tell you a curious incident in Spanish history.'

He stretched himself on a divan, and I went mechanically and sat beside him, in the half-light.

'Listen well,' he said, 'this story will give you the answer to a question you haven't been able to solve.'

'I'm listening, Captain,' I said, wondering whether he had found out our plan.

Then he told me a long story concerning the Wars of the Spanish Succession. The French under their king, Louis XIV, were in league with the Spanish against an alliance of England, Holland, and Austria. Money was needed for the war, and at that time Spain had very rich possessions in South America. A convoy of Spanish galleons, laden with gold and silver from the Indies, was on its way to Cadiz, escorted by twenty-three French warships under a certain admiral. The admiral found out that Cadiz was blockaded by the English fleet, and wanted to take the treasure into a French port. But the Spanish captains protested, and finally the admiral agreed to make for the bay of Vigo, on the north-west coast of Spain, which was not blockaded. For one reason and another, the unloading of the galleons in Vigo Bay was delayed so long that the English fleet had time to sail round after them. There was a fierce battle, but the French fleet was outnumbered. When the French admiral saw that the battle was lost, he ordered the convoy to be fired and scuttled rather than that the treasure should fall into the hands of the enemy. So the galleons sank in Vigo Bay with all their treasure on board.

The captain finished his story. For the life of me, I couldn't see much point in it.

'Well?' I said.

'Well, Mr Aronnax, we're in Vigo Bay now, and you may see for yourself.' He got up and I followed him into the dark gallery, where the shutters had been opened. The sea-bed was lit up round the ship, showing the sandy bottom. Men of the crew in diving-gear were digging out half-rotten barrels and broken cases from among the blackened wrecks of ships. From between the shattered staves ingots of gold and silver spilled out, with showers of doubloons and jewels. The sand was strewn with them. The men, laden with their precious loot, returned to the ship, unloaded and went back to their task.

I understood at last. Here, where the galleons had sunk, the captain came to fill his treasure-chests. He had made himself heir to the gold of the Incas.

He turned to me with a smile. 'Did you know there was so much wealth in the sea?' he said. 'Now you can understand how I have become a millionaire.'

'Yes,' I answered, 'I see it all now. But it's a pity that so much wealth should lie idle, when if it were shared out it could do so much good to the poor people of the world.'

The captain looked at me in hurt surprise. 'Idle!' he said indignantly. 'Do you suppose that this treasure is lost, when I am the collector of it? Do you really believe I give myself so much trouble for my own profit? Why should you think I don't put it to good use? Do you think I don't know that men suffer, that peoples are downtrodden on the earth, that there are unhappy creatures to comfort, victims to avenge? Don't you understand yet . . .?' He broke off short.

But I had understood at last. I knew now to whom he had sent that case of gold, when the *Nautilus* sailed in the waters of rebellious Crete.

28

A Vanished Continent

The next morning, February 19th, Ned came into my cabin, and indeed I had been expecting him. He was very downcast.

'Well, Ned, our luck was out last night.'

'Why did that damned captain have to stop just then?'

'He had business with his bank-manager.' I told Ned what had happened, and he was extremely put out when he realised what a chance he had lost of feathering his nest.

'Well,' he said, 'we'll get away yet! One harpoon stroke missed, that's all. Another time – perhaps this evening . . .'

'Where are we heading now?'

'I don't know.'

'Well, we'll find out the bearing, at noon.' Ned left me, and when I was dressed I went into the gallery. Our course was south-south-west, we were leaving Europe astern.

Towards noon I went up on deck, where I found Ned. There was no land in sight, only a few sails on the horizon, the sky was overcast. Ned, inwardly raging, was trying to pierce the misty distance, to see the land he longed for.

At noon the sun came out for a few moments, and the first

officer took a bearing. Then the weather drove us down again. An hour afterwards I looked at the chart, and found that we were in longitude 16 degrees 17 minutes and latitude 33 degrees 22 minutes, hundreds of miles from the nearest coast. No possibility now of escape. For my part I was not sorry, for I could get on quietly with my work.

At eleven that evening I was surprised by a visit from the captain. He asked me most graciously if I were tired from the night before, and when I said no, he went on,

'Then would you like to join me in rather a curious excursion? You haven't been on a visit to the sea-bed by night yet, will you come?'

'I should be delighted.'

'Very well, then, we'll get into diving-kit.'

I found that we were going alone. We were provided with iron-tipped sticks, but no torches, and when I asked why, the captain said, 'We don't need them.' This surprised me, but he had put on his helmet, and I followed suit. Soon we were on the sea-bed, nearly a thousand feet down.

It was almost midnight. The water was black as pitch, but the captain pointed out a reddish gleam. I had no idea what it was, but it served as a beacon, and we made directly towards it.

The sea-bed sloped upwards, and the going was sticky at first, then the ground grew stony. My feet often slipped on carpets of seaweed, but the stick helped me to keep my balance. Turning my head, I saw the submarine's lamp growing faint in the distance.

The stones on which we were walking seemed to be laid in a regular pattern, and sometimes I felt myself walking on a litter of bones which crackled under my leaden soles. Meanwhile the beacon fire grew brighter. I was mystified by this light under the sea, and wondered whether by some strange chance it could be the work of man. Might there indeed be towns under the sea, as the captain had wished? So many wonders had happened to me in the last months that I almost believed it possible.

The light was now seen to be coming from the top of a hill, but I realised that what we could see was a reflection in the water, the source of the light was over the hill-top. It was one o'clock in the morning when we reached the lowest slopes, and the path led through a great wood.

It was indeed a wood, of petrified trees, leafless, sapless, with giant pines towering here and there. It was like a coal-mine standing upright, the roots still clinging to the soil, the branches outlined against the surrounding water, with fishes swimming through them. The paths were thick with seaweed, and sea-creatures hid in the crannies of the rocks and fallen trees. I followed my guide, who knew the paths, and saw to the right and left great clearings which seemed to show the hand of man.

The trees ended about a hundred feet below the mountain top, which appeared only as a dark mass against the light behind it. We went on up the rough rocky slope, shoals of fish swam away like startled birds, and in the deep caverns I heard the noise of fearsome creatures stirring. Sometimes a pair of huge antennae barred my way, or I heard the noise of a monstrous pincer-claw snapping shut beneath my feet. The dark places bristled with thousands of shining points, they were the eyes of huge lobsters and gigantic crabs, their scuttling claws scraping like steel nails. Horrible squids waved their tentacles in the gloom.

Captain Nemo went calmly on amongst these monsters, which held no terrors for him, till we came to the hill-top. There new wonders met my eyes, for the place was strewn with ruined buildings, the work of man. I could make out the vague shapes of palaces and temples, all overgrown with sea-anemones and weeds. What could be the meaning of it all? What part of the world had sunk under the sea, and what men had built these monuments?

I was wild with curiosity, and seized the captain's arm. But he shook his head, and waved me yet farther onwards. There was a still higher summit, and in a few minutes we were standing on the topmost point of all. Now I saw the source of the beacon-light we had followed, for about fifty feet below us was a volcanic crater, belching torrents of red-hot lava. There were no flames, for flames need oxygen, but the glowing lava overflowed in streams to the foot of the mountain, steaming through the water.

A vast plain stretched away under the mountain, lit up by the burning lava. There lay a ruined city, its roofs and temples thrown down, its heavy pillars lying on the ground. Farther away were the remains of a great aqueduct, and the relics of a port which had once sheltered the merchant ships and war-galleys of a vanished people. Where were we? I longed to know at any price, and I tried to tear off my helmet. But the captain stopped me. He picked up a piece of chalky stone, and on a rock of black basalt he wrote the word, 'Atlantis'.

Then I knew. We were standing on the ruins of the ancient fabled continent, beyond the Pillars of Hercules. It had been inhabited by a powerful nation who fought against the ancient Greeks, and then, in a night and a day, it had sunk under the sea during a terrible earthquake. Only the highest peaks of its mountains still remain for us as Madeira, the Azores, the Cape Verde Islands.

I dreamed of the ancient glory of this race, and I longed for time to explore the ruined cities. While I feasted my eyes on this strange landscape, Captain Nemo, leaning against a weed-grown column, stood silent and motionless, as if turned to stone.

We stayed in that place for an hour, while the volcano rumbled under our feet, and the echoes trembled through the water. Then the moon appeared through the sea and shed a few pale rays on the submerged continent. The captain turned to go, with a last glance over the plain, and signed to me to follow him.

We went quickly down the hillside. When we had come through the wood, I saw the lamp of the *Nautilus* shining like a star. The captain walked straight ahead, and we were back on board as the first whiteness of dawn streaked the sea.

29

The Sargasso Sea

The submarine was still running south. During that day we passed through a strange part of the ocean. The main current of the Gulf Stream, as everyone knows, flows northwards from Florida round the British Isles towards Spitzbergen. There is, however, a secondary current which crosses the Atlantic towards the Azores and the African coast, then turns round on itself in a long oval and flows back towards the West Indies. This sort of lake in mid-ocean, surrounded by the warm current, is known as the Sargasso Sea. It is a great bed of floating weed, carried there by the Gulf Stream, and so dense that ships are unable to make their way through it. The submarine kept some yards below the surface while we were crossing it, so that the screw should not become entangled in the weed. We saw floating tree-trunks above us, and parts of wrecks, waterlogged keels and spars all overgrown with barnacles.

For the whole day of February 22nd we passed under the mass of weed, and saw many fish feeding there. The next day the sea was normal again.

For the following nineteen days, that is from February 23rd to

March 12th, the *Nautilus* was running in the middle of the Atlantic, with a constant speed of a hundred leagues every twenty-four hours. I believed that the captain was intending to return to the South Pacific via Cape Horn; no happy prospect for Ned, for in those great spaces of sea with hardly any islands it was hopeless to think of escape. Counsel and I began to lose courage too, and to think it unlikely that we should ever see our friends and our old life again.

While we were running south I saw very little of the captain. I knew he was working, for I often found books left open in the library. Sometimes at night I heard the melancholy strains of his organ, which he played with great feeling, while his ship slept in the deserts of ocean.

For a great part of this voyage we ran on the surface. There were very few ships to be seen, only now and then a schooner bound for India, making for the Cape of Good Hope. One day we were chased by a whaler's boats which no doubt took us for a great whale, but we dived to avoid them. I think Ned was disappointed that our steel fish was not struck to the death by one of their harpoons.

Counsel and I observed the sea-creatures, as usual, and sometimes schools of dolphins followed us for days. There were also pretty flying-fishes, with luminous mouths, which at night made loops of fire in the air, then fell back into the dark water like shooting stars.

On March 13th the *Nautilus* made experiments in deep diving which I found most interesting. We were then in latitude 54 degrees 37 minutes south by longitude 37 degrees 53 minutes west, where the ocean bed is known to be extremely deep. Captain Nemo decided to dive as deep as he could, and the shutters in the gallery were left open, so that we could see anything there was to be seen. There was no question of diving merely by filling the tanks, we had to use the hydroplanes and drive downwards on a long diagonal with the utmost power of the screw. The hydroplanes were set at an angle of forty-five degrees, the motors ran full ahead, and we dived. The captain and I watched the depth-gauge; soon we had passed through the zone of the deep-sea fishes. After an hour we had reached a depth of 3300 fathoms, and were still diving.

At about 7500 fathoms, I saw dark mountain-tops rising in the water, but these might be peaks like the summits of the Himalayas or the Alps, or even higher, and the depth of the valleys remained unknown.

The *Nautilus* went still deeper, in spite of the terrific pressure. I felt the armour plates straining, the joints warping under the force of the water. The ship was a miracle of engineering or she would have split like a nut. As we passed the slopes of these rocky summits I still saw a few shells, but by 8300 fathoms all life had ceased. The ship was then bearing a pressure of 1600 atmospheres, that is 24000 pounds to every square inch of her surface.

'What a fantastic situation!' I cried. 'To sink into these depths where no man has ever ventured before! What a pity that we can keep nothing of them but the memory!'

'Would you like to take back something better than that?' said the captain. 'We can take a photograph, if you like.' He called, and a camera was brought in. The water was brilliantly lit through the windows, the sun could not have given a better light. The *Nautilus* was brought to a standstill by the skilful manoeuvring of her screw and the hydroplanes, the camera was focused on the ocean depth, and an exposure was taken.

The negative came out very well, it was possible to see those rocks and caves and the whole extraordinary underwater landscape.

Then the captain turned to me and said, 'Let's surface again, the ship has been exposed to this pressure for long enough. Hold hard!'

I was wondering why he had warned me when I found myself flat on the floor. At the captain's order the ship shot upwards like a cork. In four minutes she travelled the four leagues to the surface, leapt into the air like a flying-fish, and fell back with a splash like a cloudburst.

30

The Icepack

The southward voyage continued. Was the captain making for the South Pole? Surely not, for all attempts so far to reach it had failed. The season was very late too, for March 13th in the Antarctic is the beginning of the equinoctial period.

On March 14th I saw floating ice at latitude 55 degrees. The submarine was surfaced, and on the south horizon was a brilliant white band, which whalers call the 'iceblink'. It shows the presence of pack-ice. Ned had hunted in the Arctic seas, and was familiar with icebergs, but Counsel and I had never seen them before. We were thrilled by these great blocks of ice, shining with green and violet lights, with sea-birds resting on them in their thousands.

As the floating ice grew thicker, the captain often stood beside the helmsman, steering the ship with great skill through narrow channels. It was very cold, the thermometer stood at several degrees below zero, but we were warmly dressed in furs from the seal and the polar bear. Inside the ship, the air was kept warm by the heating system.

On March 16th about eight in the morning we crossed the

Antarctic Circle. There was ice all round us, but the captain managed to find a way through.

'But where's he going?' I said.

'Straight ahead,' said Counsel. 'After all, he'll have to stop when he can't go any farther.'

'I wouldn't count on that!'

And indeed I found this polar expedition exciting. The ice took mysterious and ever-changing shapes, and when the bergs turned over the ship was tossed as if by a hurricane. Sometimes I thought we were imprisoned in the ice, but always the captain spied out veins of pale blue water along which we could make our way. At last, however, on March 15th our way was completely blocked. The pack-ice had turned into a close-knit icefield. Then the captain threw his *Nautilus* against the mass like a battering-ram, and the sharp prow cut a channel, while the broken ice crashed round us, shooting into the air and falling like hail. Sometimes the ship rose on top of the ice and crushed it, sometimes by pitching she split it into great rents.

During those days, there were violent squalls and heavy fogs, and sometimes the snow froze so hard on deck that it had to be chipped off with picks. When the temperature fell five degrees below zero, all the exposed parts of the ship were coated with ice. As we drew still southward, the magnetic pole threw the compass needle out, and it wavered like a mad thing.

Then at last, on March 18th, the *Nautilus* found herself definitely imprisoned in the ice. There was no way of escape, there was a solid barrier of impenetrable ice before us, and it was the same astern, for the ice had closed after our passage. The sun came out for a short time about noon, and the captain was able to take a fairly good bearing, which showed our position as longitude 51 degrees 30 minutes by latitude 67 degrees 39 minutes south.

We lay, surrounded by ice, and all noise seemed to have been frozen too. Already the young ice was forming round the ship, and if she stayed there motionless for long she would soon be frozen solid into the mass. Then the captain came up on deck.

'Well, Professor, what do you think of the situation?'

'I'm afraid we're stuck, Captain.'

'You always take such a gloomy view. You see nothing but difficulties. I tell you, the *Nautilus* will free herself, and will go even farther!'

'Farther south?'

'Yes, to the Pole!'

'To the Pole!' I stammered.

'Yes, to the South Pole. You know my ship will go wherever I wish.'

It occurred to me then to ask him whether he had perhaps already discovered the Pole.

'Not yet. We'll discover it together. I've never been so far south, but we'll succeed where others have failed.'

'I should like to believe you,' I said rather sarcastically. 'Give wings to your *Nautilus,* fly over the ice to the Pole!'

'Not over the ice,' he said calmly, 'under it.' I gasped. 'I see we're beginning to understand one another,' he went on with a half-smile. 'You already see how it can be done. If there's land at the Pole, the *Nautilus* will stop, but if it's open sea, she'll go right to the Pole!'

'Yes, of course, the sea can't freeze very deep on account of its density.'

'And as these ice cliffs are not above three hundred feet high, they can't be more than nine hundred feet deep, as there's always three-quarters of an iceberg below the surface. Well, what's nine hundred feet to the *Nautilus*?'

'What, indeed?'

'The only difficulty will be that we shall probably have to stay submerged for several days without renewing our air.'

'No difficulty at all,' I said, 'you have vast reserve tanks of compressed air.'

'Good, very good, Professor. Now, so that you can't accuse me of foolhardiness, I'll tell you all my doubts in advance.'

'Have you still any doubts?'

'Only one. Suppose there is sea at the South Pole, and it's frozen solid, we may not be able to surface!'

'Have you forgotten that the *Nautilus* has a steel spur fitted to her bows, and can't she be driven up through the ice?'

'Well, you're outdoing me in rashness now!' He called his first officer, and they spoke quickly together in their language.

When I told Counsel of the captain's plan, he took it all quite calmly, but with Ned it was a different story.

'You and your Captain Nemo,' he said, 'you make me cry!'

'But we're going to the Pole, Ned.'

'Maybe, but you won't come back.' So he went to his cabin, to stop himself doing a mischief, he said.

In the meantime, preparations were made for the bold attempt. The high-powered pumps stored air under pressure in the tanks. Ten men of the crew climbed on to the hull and hacked the ship clear of the ice with picks, which did not take long, for the young ice was still thin. Then the captain ordered the deck to be cleared for diving. I threw a last glance at the daylight and went below. The tanks were filled with water, and the *Nautilus* dived.

I went into the gallery with Counsel. We watched the needle of the depth-gauge as it moved round the dial. At about 900 feet, as the captain had predicted, we floated under the wavy surface of the ice. But the ship dived still deeper, till she reached 2400 feet.

'We shall get through!' said Counsel.

'I think we shall!'

Now that she could move freely, the *Nautilus* was set directly for the Pole. She should reach it in forty hours, if she kept up her speed of twenty-two knots. We stayed for some time in the gallery, looking out at the lighted sea, but there were no fish in those imprisoned waters.

The next day, March 19th, at five in the morning, I went back to the gallery. The electric log showed that the *Nautilus* had slackened speed, she was coming up towards the surface. There was a bump as she hit the bottom of the ice-bank. The depth-gauge read 3000 feet, which meant that there were 4000 feet of ice above us, of which 1000 were above the surface of the sea. The ice was therefore higher than it had been when we dived, not a comforting thought.

Several times that day the ship tried the same experiment, and once or twice I noticed that the ice was even thicker. However, at eight in the evening, the ice was found to be getting thinner – between 12 and 15 hundred feet. This was something, but it was still a terrible thickness. The air supply should have been renewed four hours before, it was very stuffy, but still bearable. I got up several times in the night to find out how we were getting on, and at three there were only 150 feet between us and the surface. I stayed by the depth-gauge, which showed that we were gradually climbing, until at six in the morning the door of the gallery opened, and the captain came in.

'The open sea!' he said.

31

The South Pole

I rushed up on deck, and filled my lungs with long draughts of cold fresh air. The sea! Only a few scattered icebergs, and the clear water stretching away in the distance. The air was filled with birds and the sea with fish swimming in the green water, the temperature was three degrees below zero. It was like spring after the long imprisonment under the terrible ice, which stretched away in the distance astern.

'Are we at the Pole?' I asked in excitement.

'I don't know,' said the captain. 'At noon I shall take a bearing, if the mist lifts.'

Ten miles to the southward lay an islet, which we reached in an hour. We sailed round it, and found that it was separated by a narrow channel from a considerable stretch of land. This might well be the continent which explorers have supposed to lie at the South Pole.

The *Nautilus* stopped three cables from the shore, and the boat was launched. The captain, two of the crew carrying the instruments, Counsel and I took our places in the boat. I hadn't seen Ned, who was keeping out of the way. We reached the land, and Counsel was about to jump out when I stopped him.

'It's for you to set foot first on this land, Captain,' I said.

'Yes, and I'll do so willingly, since no human being has ever set foot here before.' He leapt ashore and climbed to the top of a little headland, and there, standing with folded arms, he seemed to take possession of this antarctic land.

After a few minutes he called to us to follow. Counsel and I stepped ashore and wandered round the island. The ground was volcanic, there were few plants but lichens, but there was plenty of life, especially in the air. There were thousands of birds of different kinds, wheeling above our heads, and penguins crowded on the rocks, watching us pass without fear.

But the mist did not lift. I went to find the captain, and came upon him leaning on a rock, looking gloomily at the sky. Noon arrived without a sign of the sun, and the mist changed into snow.

He started to make for the boat. 'We'll try again tomorrow,' he said.

The snowstorm lasted all that day, but by the next day it had stopped, and the weather looked a little clearer. Counsel and I went on shore at eight, and had another interesting scramble. We went further afield this time, and found a colony of seals, which looked at us with their great soft eyes and were not a bit afraid of us, since they had never seen men before. Later on we found a herd of walrus, bellowing with joy as they played together on the shore.

It was drawing near to noon, and I wanted to watch the captain take his bearing, if he could, though I very much feared the sun would not show itself that day either. We walked back towards the submarine, and found the captain on shore with his instruments. But we were unlucky again, for noon passed without the sun piercing the clouds. The next day, March 21st, would be the equinox, and therefore the last chance of finding out where we were. For the sun would be visible for the last time tomorrow, before disappearing below the horizon for the six months' polar night.

When I mentioned this to the captain, he said, 'True enough, Professor, but if the sun does appear at noon tomorrow, it will be very easy to take our bearings.'

'How then?'

'I need only use my chronometer. If tomorrow at noon, the sun's circle, allowing for refraction, is cut exactly in two by the north horizon, it will mean that I am at the South Pole.'

The next day the weather looked a little better. I went ashore in the morning; I wanted to take Ned with me, but he refused to come, preferring to stay brooding in gloomy silence in his cabin. Perhaps it was just as well, as the sight of all those seals would have been too much for him.

The *Nautilus* had moved several miles out to sea in the night, so that we had a longer trip in the boat. I saw many whales, gathered in these calm waters to escape the pitiless whalers.

When we landed at nine, the sky was lifting. The captain made for a hill which was to serve as his observatory. The ground was rough with broken lava and pumice, and sulphurous smoke jetted up from blowholes. The captain might be unused to walking on land, but he climbed that hill like a chamois-hunter, leaving me far behind.

From the hill-top we looked out over the great sea stretching to the north horizon, with snowfields at our feet, and overhead a clear, pale sky. To the north, the disc of the sun was already cut by the horizon.

The captain took a careful observation of the height by means of the barometer, for he would have to make allowance for it. At a quarter to twelve, the sun, then seen only by refraction, showed like a gold disc and shed its last rays over the deserted continent. The captain watched through a special glass, which corrected the refraction by means of a mirror, while the sun sloped downwards under the horizon. I held the chronometer, my heart beating wildly. If the sun showed as a half-circle exactly at noon, we were at the Pole.

'Noon!' I cried.

'The South Pole,' replied the captain gravely, handing me the telescope. I saw the half-circle of the sun over the horizon. Then its last rays touched the heights and the shadows advanced up the hillsides.

The captain put his hand on my shoulder.

'Since the year 1600,' he said, 'explorers of all the seafaring nations have been trying to find the Pole. Now I, Captain Nemo, this 21st March 1868, have reached the South Pole, and I take possession of this part of the earth's surface equal to a sixth of the recognised continents.'

'In whose name, Captain?'

'In my own name, sir!' With these words, he unfurled and planted a black flag with an N in gold embroidered on it. Then turning towards the last rays of the sun, he spoke:

'Farewell, sun! Sink under this free ocean, and let the six months' night fall on my new domain!'

32

Imprisoned in the Ice

The next morning at six the *Nautilus* made ready to leave her anchorage. It was very cold, the stars shone brilliantly, among them the Southern Cross. The wind rose, and it looked as if the water were about to freeze over. The tanks were filled, and the submarine dived slowly. She made for the north at a depth of a thousand feet, and towards evening, she was already under the ice.

About three in the morning I was awakened by a violent shock. I rolled out of bed and made my way into the gallery, lighted as usual from the ceiling. There I found everything topsy-turvy, furniture overturned, pictures on the port side hanging away from the wall, The ship was evidently lying with a strong list to starboard, and quite still. I heard a confused noise of voices outside, but the captain did not appear. Then Ned and Counsel rushed in.

'What's happened?' I asked them.

'That's what we were going to ask,' said Counsel. I saw from the depth-gauge that we were a thousand feet below the surface.

We stayed in the gallery, Ned raging and fuming as usual.

After some time the captain came in, looking rather anxious. He consulted the instruments, then stood looking at the globe. He turned towards me, and I asked him, 'An incident, Captain?'

'No, an accident this time,' he answered. He told me that an iceberg, turning over, had hit the submarine, then, floating upwards, had raised the ship with it so that she was now lying on her side on the berg. The crew were at that moment trying to free the ship by emptying her tanks. She was indeed rising, as the depth-gauge showed, but the ice was rising with her. It was certainly an anxious moment, for if nothing stopped the iceberg the ship would be crushed between it and the bottom of the ice-pack.

The captain kept his eyes on the depth-gauge. The ship had risen a hundred and fifty feet since the collision, but she was still lying on a list. Suddenly there was a slight movement through the hull, she was righting herself. The floor and the walls gradually came back to normal, in ten minutes we were on an even keel.

'A narrow escape!' said Counsel.

'Don't speak too soon!' said Ned.

Then the shutters opened, and we all looked through the windows. We were indeed floating, but ten yards away from either beam there was a dazzling wall of ice. Above us was the pack-ice, below us the iceberg, which as it floated upwards had become wedged between the walls of a crevice in the pack-ice. We were therefore floating in a narrow tunnel of water surrounded by ice on all sides. We should no doubt be able to get out at one or the other end of the tunnel, and go on with our voyage some hundred feet lower down.

In the meantime we looked at the brilliant spectacle on either side of us. The ice under the rays of the lamp shone with the most incredible colours, like sapphires, emeralds and diamonds blazing in glory.

'How beautiful!' cried Counsel.

'Yes,' I said, 'it's, a wonderful sight, isn't it, Ned?'

'Yes, curse it,' answered Ned, 'it is, it's superb. I hate to say it, but I've never seen anything so magnificent in my life. But depend on me, we'll pay for this, the Lord never meant us poor mortals to see such sights as this.'

Unfortunately it seemed Ned was right. Suddenly Counsel cried out, clapping his hands to his eyes.

'I'm dazzled,' he gasped, 'blinded!' I looked at the window in spite of myself, and in a moment I was blinded too. The *Nautilus* was now going ahead, and the ice-walls had turned into streaks of dazzling light. Then the shutters were closed, but it was some time before our eyes recovered.

At five in the morning there was a slight shock ahead, and I realised that the ship must have struck a block of ice. Then she started to reverse.

'We're going backwards!' said Counsel.

'I suppose the tunnel is closed ahead, so we shall have to get out astern. That's all.' But I didn't feel quite as confident as I sounded.

The ship went astern till at eight-twenty-five there was a second slight shock, aft this time. We looked at each other in silence. Then the captain came in.

'The way's blocked to the south?' I asked.

'Yes,' he said. 'We're shut in.'

33

Lack of Air

Ned banged on the table. Counsel said not a word. I looked at the captain. He was standing, calm as usual, his arms folded.

'Gentlemen,' he said, 'there are two ways of dying in our present situation.' He looked like a lecturer addressing a class. 'The first is to be crushed to death. The second is to be suffocated. I'm not considering starving, since our provisions will certainly last as long as we shall.'

'We shan't be suffocated,' I said, 'since the air-tanks are full.'

'Yes, but they only hold two days' supply. We've been submerged for thirty-six hours already, and it's time our air was renewed. In forty-eight hours, our reserves will be used up.'

'Well then, we must get out within forty-eight hours!'

'We're trying it already. I shall ground the ship on the bottom of the channel, and my men will try to hack a way through the ice. We'll start by making borings to find the thinnest place.' He went out.

The tanks were filled and the *Nautilus* sank slowly till she rested on the ice.

'We're in a tight spot,' I said. 'We must all pull together now.'

The Canadian grinned. 'I guess I'll have to let my private war ride,' he said. 'I'm handy with a pick.'

'Good man,' I said. 'Come along.' I went with him to the room where the men were getting into diving-kit. Ned's offer was not refused, and he was soon ready. The compressed-air tubes were fastened on to their backs.

Counsel and I went back to the gallery to watch, and soon we saw a dozen seamen set foot on the ice, Ned towering above them. The captain was with them, and they started making borings. The side walls turned out to be enormously thick, and we knew that the roof was about 1200 feet high. There remained the floor, which proved to be about thirty feet thick. This, then, was the only way. It would be necessary to cut out a hole the size of the *Nautilus,* and to do this we should have to shift about 7000 cubic yards of ice.

As it would be very difficult to cut round the ship herself, the captain marked out a huge trench about eight yards from the port beam. Then the men attacked it at several points at once. It was strange to see the ice blocks floating upwards when they had been hacked out.

After two hours, Ned and the others came back exhausted. A second shift took their place, among whom were Counsel and I, under the first officer's command. When I came back after two hours' work for rest and food, I noticed a great difference between the pure air I had been breathing from the tube and the foul atmosphere of the *Nautilus*, loaded with carbon dioxide gas.

The plan seemed hopeless. If we went on working at our present rate, we should need five nights and four days more to finish the job, and our air supply would be used up in two days. The next time I went on the shift, I noticed a new danger. It was very cold, and in the parts of the ditch where we were not working the water was freezing again. When I came back on board, I mentioned this to the captain.

'I know,' he said, 'but I don't see what we can do about it. We shall just have to work faster than it can freeze.'

I was glad when my shift came round again; it was good to have this hard work to keep my mind off our plight, and also the working-party had fresh air to breathe. That night the captain had to open the tanks and let some air into the ship, or we should never have wakened again.

The next day when I went on the shift I noticed to my horror that the side walls and the ice ceiling were thickening visibly. We had hacked about half-way through the ten yards below us, but it looked as if we were going to be frozen in before we could make our way out below. At that moment the captain, organising the work and wielding a pick himself, came near me, and I touched his arm and pointed to the walls. The starboard barrier was now less than four yards from the hull.

The captain signed to me to follow him, and we went back on board. We took off our kit and went into the gallery.

'We shall have to try something desperate,' he said. 'Not only are the walls closing in on us, but there's not more than ten feet of water to fore and aft.'

'How much more air have we?' I asked.

'The day after tomorrow the tanks will be empty.'

I felt a cold sweat breaking out over my body. For five days, from March 22nd to 26th, we had been living on our reserves of air. The captain was silent, thinking. Then suddenly I heard him murmur, 'Boiling water!'

'What!'

'Well, why not? It might work. We're in a very narrow space. Let's try it!'

We went to the galley, where there were huge boilers for

distilling drinking-water. These were filled and the electric power was turned full on. Soon the water was boiling, and a scalding jet was pumped into the sea, while a constant stream of cold water was fed into the boilers.

In three hours the temperature of the sea had risen from minus seven degrees to minus six. In two more hours a further two degrees were gained.

'We'll do it!' I cried.

'I think we shall,' said the captain. 'We shan't be crushed, only suffocated.'

During the night the temperature rose still further to one degree below zero. It couldn't be raised any higher, but since sea-water doesn't freeze above minus two degrees, we were safe from that danger.

But the air on board grew worse and worse. On March 27th there remained only four yards of ice below us, but that was forty-eight hours' work, and the air supply couldn't be renewed. By three in the afternoon, I was overcome by a terrible heaviness, and lay gasping for breath, almost unconscious. Counsel, who was suffering the same pains, leaned over me and took my hand, and I heard him murmuring,

'Oh, if only I could stop breathing to leave more air for the master!'

During that time we all rushed with eagerness to take our turn on the shift. The work was hard, but we could breathe, since what air still remained was reserved for the working-party. But no man tried to keep on the shift longer than the allotted time; as soon as it was over, every man passed his breathing-apparatus to his mate on the next team.

There were only two more yards to go. The next night and day were dreadful, we all had violent headaches and frequent blackouts, accompanied in some cases by a rattling in the throat.

It was the sixth day of our imprisonment. The captain, whose calmness and energy had never flagged, made up his mind to crush the last layer of ice by the dead weight of the ship. The water-tanks were partly emptied till she floated, then she was hauled over the great ditch we had dug. Then her tanks were filled again and she sank into the hole. The whole crew came aboard and the hatch was shut. The ship lay on less than a yard of ice, pierced with many bore-holes. The valves of the tanks were opened full, and the water rushed in. We waited, listening, still hoping. In spite of the buzzing in my head, I heard the ice groaning under us, then suddenly with a mighty crack it gave way. Then the *Nautilus* sank like lead in the water, and I grasped the hand of Counsel standing beside me.

The pumps set to work to drive out the surplus water, and our dive was halted, then the motors were set full ahead, and we made all speed for the north.

But how long would it last? Yet another day? I should be dead before then. I lay on a sofa in the library, my lips blue, unable to move. I knew that I was dying . . .

Suddenly a waft of fresh air filled my lungs. Had we surfaced? No, Ned and Counsel had found a little air in one of the tubes, and were holding the pipe to my nose while they were suffocating themselves. I tried to push it away, but they held my hands. I looked at the clock, it was eleven in the morning. It must be March 28th. The *Nautilus* was running at the terrific speed of thirty-five knots.

Where was the captain? Where were the crew? Were they all dead? The depth-gauge read twenty feet only. Couldn't we break through? At any rate, we were going to try it. I felt the ship sinking by the stern, then with the motor full ahead she attacked the ice-field like a battering-ram. She shoved, then drew back and shoved again, and at last with a final spurt she shot up through the ice and over its surface, crushing it with her weight.

The hatch was opened, and fresh air rushed into the ship.

34

From Cape Horn to the Amazon

How I got up on deck, I have no idea. Perhaps Ned carried me. But there we were, all three, filling our lungs with the good air of the sea.

'Ah,' said Counsel at last, 'how good it is, oxygen! Enough for us all and to spare.' Ned said nothing, but opened his jaws wide enough to swallow a shark.

Soon we were ourselves again, and when I looked round I was astonished to see that we were alone on deck. Not a man of the crew, not even the captain. These strange seamen were satisfied with the air now circulating inside the submarine, none of them came up to guzzle it like us.

My first words were to thank my mates. They had saved my life during those last hours, and I was overcome with gratitude.

'Never mind all that,' said Ned. 'Now, what about getting away from this confounded ship? Are we going into the Pacific or the Atlantic, that is, away from shipping or towards it?'

The *Nautilus* made good speed. Soon we crossed the Antarctic Circle, and set course for Cape Horn. We were off the southernmost point of the American continent on March 31st, at seven in the evening.

Then all our past suffering under the ice was forgotten. We thought only of the future. The captain did not appear, either on deck or in the gallery. The first officer took our daily bearings and marked them on the chart, so that I could follow our progress. I saw then to my joy that we were taking the Atlantic route, and I told the others.

'Good,' said Ned. 'Now I suppose we'll make for the North Pole. But we'll get away before then.'

We made our way up the east coast of South America, sometimes on the surface, sometimes submerged. I saw Tierra del Fuego, then the Falkland Islands, then on April 3rd we passed the mouth of La Plata river. We kept on northwards, having made 16,000 leagues since the start of our voyage in the Japanese waters. We rounded Cape San Roque, the easternmost point of South America, and the *Nautilus* spent two days in very deep diving. Then on April 11th she rose to the surface, and we found ourselves off the mouth of the vast estuary of the Amazon.

We had had no chance of escape during this voyage, for the ship had made great speed and kept well out to sea. But here we were fifty miles from French Guiana, where we could easily have found refuge. However, there was a high wind and a heavy sea, and even Ned did not think of attempting to take the boat.

For the two days of April 11th and 12th, the submarine kept on the surface, and the nets brought in a wonderful catch. Counsel and I were delighted with this chance of studying the fish of these regions, and indeed, poor Counsel had good cause to remember one fish in particular.

One of the nets brought in a large, flat ray, weighing something like forty pounds. It was flapping about on deck, struggling to get back into the sea, when Counsel, who had taken a fancy to it, rushed forward and seized it in both hands. He fell back on deck paralysed, crying out,

'Master! Master! Help me!' It was the first time the poor fellow had spoken to me except in the third person!

Ned and I pulled him up and massaged him, and when he came back to his senses, he started to classify the fish.

'Family of rays, species torpedo!' he murmured.

'Yes, that was a torpedo-ray,' I said. 'A fine shock it gave you.'

'Well, I'll have my revenge,' said Counsel, 'I'll eat that fish.' And eat it he did, in pure spite, for it was as tough as an old boot.

At the mouth of the Maroni river, we caught half-a-dozen manatees, or sea-cows of a different kind from the dugong. It was pure slaughter, for these peaceful creatures did not try to escape, but their flesh was needed for food. After provisioning the ship we left the neighbourhood of the Amazon and made for the open sea again.

35

The Giant Squids

For some days the *Nautilus* kept to the open sea, far out from the Gulf of Mexico and the Caribbean. These frequented waters evidently did not suit the captain. Ned raged as usual, but there was nothing to be done about it.

On April 20th, I was with Ned and Counsel in the gallery, watching some gigantic sea-plants through the windows, when Ned noticed a violent shaking amongst them.

'These seaweeds are large enough to be a breeding-ground for squids,' I said, 'and I shouldn't be surprised if we saw some of those monsters.'

'What, inkfish,' said Counsel, 'nothing but inkfish?'

'No, giant squids I mean, of vast size. But I don't see anything.'

'I'm sorry, then,' said Counsel, 'for I'd like to meet one of those creatures face to face. I've heard they can pull ships down to the bottom of the sea, krakens they call them.'

'There's no such thing,' said Ned. We had a long discussion about them, and I told them all I had ever heard about these creatures, some of which are said to be six feet long in the body, which would give them tentacles of twenty-seven feet.

'How long did you say?' asked Ned.

'Wasn't it about six feet?' said Counsel, who was looking through the window.

'Exactly,' I answered.

'Did it have eight tentacles on its head, like a nest of serpents?'

'Certainly.'

'With huge eyes?'

'Yes.'

'And a mouth like a parrot's beak?'

'Yes, Counsel.'

'Will the master take a look through the window, then?'

Ned rushed to the glass. 'What a loathsome brute!' he cried. I looked too, and started back in horror. Before my eyes was a hideous monster, swimming backwards with enormous speed towards the ship, staring with its huge glassy eyes. It had eight legs growing out of its head, twisting about like the Gorgon's snaky locks. I could see the undersides of them studded with suckers, especially when they were stuck to the glass. Its horny beak opened and shut, and from it darted a hard tongue armed with several rows of sharp teeth. Its bloated body must have weighed twenty tons. Its colour changed from livid grey to reddish brown as it grew more and more angry; no doubt it was annoyed by the submarine, since it couldn't make the slightest impression on the armour-plated hull. These creatures have great vitality, since they have three hearts, and the power to grow limbs again if they lose them.

I didn't want to miss the chance of studying the animal, so I overcame my disgust, and taking out a pencil started to make a drawing of it. Then more of them came up, till I could count seven. They swam along with the ship, and I heard the grating of their beaks against the steel.

Suddenly the *Nautilus* stopped with a shudder throughout her hull.

'What have we hit?' I asked.

'Anyway we're floating,' said Ned. We were indeed free in the water, but the movements of the screw had ceased. Then the captain and the first officer came into the gallery.

It was some time since I had seen the captain, and he looked grave. Without speaking to us, perhaps without seeing us, he went to the window, looked at the squids and spoke a few words to the first officer, who went out. Soon the shutters were closed. I went up to the captain.

'A curious collection of squids,' I said, as if my interest were purely scientific.

'Yes, indeed, Professor,' he answered, 'and we're going to fight them hand to hand.' I looked at him in horror. 'The screw's stopped,' he went on, 'I think one of these brutes has got caught up in the mechanism.'

'What are you going to do, then?'

'Surface and massacre this vermin.'

'Not very easy.'

'No. My electric bullets can do nothing against this soft flesh, since there's not enough resistance to explode them. Never mind, we'll go for them with hatchets.'

'And harpoons,' said Ned, 'if you'll let me join you?'

'Certainly, Ned.'

We all went to the central ladder, where we found ten of the crew armed with boarding axes. Counsel and I took one each, while Ned seized a harpoon. The ship had surfaced, and a seaman at the top of the ladder was unscrewing the hatch. As soon as the screws were undone, the hatch flew open violently, then a long tentacle slid down like a snake, while twenty more waved overhead. The captain struck off the mighty arm with a blow from his axe, and it slithered twisting down the ladder.

As we were all waiting our turns to get up on deck, a horrible thing happened. Two more tentacles waved through the air, and swooping down on the seaman at the top of the ladder carried him off out of our sight. The captain dashed out with a cry, and we followed.

A ghastly sight met our eyes. The wretched man, bound in the coils of the arm and held by its suckers, was swinging in the air at the monster's mercy. With choking breath he cried out, 'Help! Help!' These words, spoken in French, struck me to the quick; so I had a countryman on board!

The man was lost. How could he be rescued from that dreadful grasp? The captain flung himself on the monster and struck off another arm, while the first officer was struggling fiercely against the rest of the brutes climbing all over the ship. The seamen lashed out with their hatchets, and we three buried our weapons in the masses of flesh. At one moment I thought the victim would be rescued; seven of the beast's arms had been cut off, and only the one which held him remained, waving in the air. But as the captain and the first officer threw themselves against the final arm, the squid shot out a column of black ink from the pouch in its belly. We were blinded, and when at last we could look up again the animal had disappeared along with my wretched countryman!

We flung ourselves raging against the rest of the monsters. There were ten or twelve of them clambering over the deck and the hull. We rolled pell-mell among these snaky arms in torrents of blood and black ink. Ned was thrusting his harpoon into the brutes' eyes, when suddenly he was thrown down by one of the monsters which had come up behind him. Its beak opened over his body, I sprang to his rescue, but the captain was before me, and buried his axe between the huge mandibles. Ned leapt up and plunged his harpoon deep into the triple heart of the squid.

'I owed you that!' said the captain. Ned smiled.

The battle had lasted a quarter of an hour. The remaining monsters gave up and disappeared under the waves, leaving us to ourselves. The captain stood still near the lamp, looking at the sea which had swallowed one of his men, while tears ran silently down his stern cheeks.

36

An Interview with Captain Nemo

I shall never forget that fight with the giant squids, and the terrible fate of the seaman. The captain was overwhelmed by grief. This was the second of his companions to be lost since we had come on board, and what a death! It did not bear thinking about. For my part, the man's last cry was still ringing in my ears, that cry in his mother-tongue which he had remembered in his desperate need.

The captain went back to his cabin, and I did not see him again for some days. During that time the ship wandered without a set course, like a floating corpse, reflecting her commander's grief and despair. He did not seem to be able to leave that water which had swallowed one of his men.

Then on May 1st the submarine was set on her former north-bound course. We followed the current of the Gulf Stream, that river in the sea, warmer and salter than the surrounding water. On May 8th we were thirty miles off the coast of North Carolina. No watch was kept, and it seemed that an escape might be possible. But the weather was very bad, for we were in the zone of gales and cyclones, and to take the boat would have been certain death.

Ned realised this fully, and it did nothing to soothe his homesickness and his gnawing desire to escape. At last he could keep quiet no longer.

'I can't go on like this,' he said to me. 'Your Captain Nemo is making for the North Pole now, and I'm damned if I'll follow him there.'

'But what can we do, Ned, with the sea like this?'

'We must speak to him. When I think that in a few days we'll be off Nova Scotia, at the mouth of the St Lawrence, my own river, near Quebec, my native town! I'm sick with anger, I'm stifling here, I'd rather throw myself into the sea!'

I saw that Ned's self-control was at an end, and I too was getting thoroughly tired of the voyage. It was seven months since we had had any news of the world. The captain kept himself apart with his own gloomy thoughts, and I felt I couldn't bear much more of it. Only Counsel took everything with his Flemish calm.

'Very well, Ned,' I said at last. 'I'll speak to the captain.'

'When?'

'When I meet him.'

'Mr Aronnax, do you want me to go and find him myself?'

'No, I'll go. Tomorrow . . .'

'Today,' said he.

'All right. I'll go at once.'

I went back to my cabin. I heard the captain's steps in his room next door, and thought I had better get it over. I knocked, there was no answer. I knocked again, then opened the door and went in. The captain was bowed over his work-table, he hadn't heard me. I went closer, he raised his head, frowned, and snapped out,

'You! What do you want?'

'To speak to you, Captain.'

'I'm busy, can't you see? I don't disturb you, why can't you leave me alone?' Not a very happy beginning, but I was not to be put off.

'Sir,' I said coldly, 'I must speak to you urgently.'

'Well, then, what is it?' said he sarcastically. 'Have you made some wonderful discovery that has escaped me?' Then he pointed to a manuscript open on the table, and said in a more serious tone: 'This is a manuscript written in several languages, it contains the results of my researches. It will be signed with my name, and I shall add to it the story of my life. It will then be sealed in an unsinkable case. The last survivor of my crew will throw it into the sea, and it will float wherever the waves carry it.'

The man's name and his history! Would they then come to light one day? But I spoke quickly,

'Can't you find a better way of preserving your work? You, or one of your men, could carry it . . .'

'Never!' he burst out.

'But I and my companions will gladly take this manuscript, if you will give us our liberty . . .'

'Liberty!' he cried, jumping up.

'Yes, and that's why I've come to see you. We've been on board for seven months; do you mean to keep us here for ever?'

'As I told you seven months ago,' he said, 'no one who comes on board the *Nautilus* can ever leave.'

'That's slavery!'

'Call it what you like.'

'Captain,' I went on, 'we're strangers here. You and your men are bound to the *Nautilus* by some mystery of which we know nothing. We shall never be at home here. Let us go. Have you never considered the effect of this imprisonment on a violent and passionate nature like Ned Land's, or to what lengths you may drive him?'

'What do I care what Ned Land may do? I didn't invite him

on board, it's no pleasure to me to keep him. As for you, Mr Aronnax, you should understand, even when I keep silence. I have no more to say. Don't speak to me of this again, for I won't listen.'

I left him alone. After that conversation our relationship was very strained.

'Now we know where we are,' said Ned, when I had spoken to him. 'We'll get no help from that man. The *Nautilus* is close to Long Island. We'll escape, whatever the weather.'

But the sky grew threatening, it looked as if a hurricane were blowing up. Clouds ran swiftly across the horizon, the sea rose, the barometer dropped very low.

The storm broke, next day, May 9th, as we were level with Long Island. Instead of diving, the captain took the strange humour of riding it out on the surface. The wind blew hard from the south-west, and by three in the afternoon it had reached gale force. The captain stayed on deck, lashing himself round the waist so that he should not be swept into the sea. I did the same, watching the storm and the man who rode it. The waves rose to giant heights, the *Nautilus* pitched and tossed between the mountains and valleys of the sea. Towards five, a torrential rain fell. The hurricane was blowing nearly a hundred miles an hour, strong enough to blow down houses and shift heavy artillery. But the steel shuttle of the submarine, with neither mast nor rigging, was unharmed in the fury of the elements.

The storm grew even more violent in the night. As the daylight faded I saw a big ship labouring to keep afloat; she disappeared soon in the shadows.

At ten, the whole sky was on fire with lightning playing across it in dazzling forks. I was unable to bear its brilliance, but the captain looked the lightning full in the face, as if breathing in the soul of the storm. There was a noise as of all hell let loose, thunderclaps mixed with the roaring of the waves and the wind. It was blowing from all quarters of the sky at once. As the steel bows of the *Nautilus* shot above the water in her ghastly pitching they sent up showers of sparks. Worn out, I crawled to the hatch. I managed to get it open and went below. The captain came in about midnight. I heard the sound of the tanks being filled, then the submarine dived. It was not till she reached a depth of a hundred and fifty feet that she was beyond the reach of the hurly-burly above.

What infinite peace at those depths! No one would have thought that a hurricane was raging on the surface.

37

In the Atlantic

The storm threw us to the north-east, far from New York and the St Lawrence river. Ned in despair shut himself up like the captain, while Counsel and I stayed together.

From May 15th to 28th we were crossing the Atlantic. We passed through the cod fisheries of the Newfoundland Bank, then followed the line of the transatlantic cable. At one point, 1400 fathoms deep, we saw the cable lying on the sea-bed, all overgrown with shells and sea-creatures and encrusted with a stony deposit.

On May 28th we were 120 miles from the Irish coast, and I saw Cape Clear and Fastnet Beacon, which lights ships from Glasgow and Liverpool. I wondered whether the *Nautilus* would venture into the English Channel, and Ned was on tenterhooks. On May 30th we passed within sight of Land's End, between that point and the Scillies. But the ship did not turn east along the Channel. Instead, she swept the sea in circles, as if searching for some particular point. At noon, the captain came up on deck to take the bearing himself. He did not speak to me, and seemed more gloomy than ever. The next day, June 1st, the ship was still circling, and the captain came on deck again. The sea was calm, the sky clear. Eight miles to the east there was a large steamship on the horizon. She flew no flag, and I couldn't make out her nationality.

The captain took his bearing with great care, then said,

'It's here!' and went below. I didn't know whether he had seen the ship, which seemed to be making towards us.

I returned to the gallery, and the *Nautilus* dived. She went straight down, and a few minutes afterwards she rested on the sea-bed in 420 fathoms. The lights in the gallery went out, and the shutters were opened. I looked through the windows, and to starboard I saw a great hump, like a heap of ruins encrusted with white shells like snow. As I looked, I could make out the shrouded form of a ship's hull, shorn of her masts, which had gone down by the bows. She must have been there a long time to be so crusted over.

I was wondering why the *Nautilus* had come to visit this dead ship, when I heard the captain's voice speaking slowly beside me.

'This ship was once called the *Marseillais*. She carried seventy-four guns and was launched in 1762. After a glorious career her name was changed by the French Republic and in 1794 she was part of the escort of a convoy of grain-ships from America. Then she met with English warships in this very place. There was a heroic fight, and with her three masts shot away, water in her powder-magazine, a third of her crew out of action, she preferred to scuttle herself with her three hundred and fifty men rather than surrender. So they nailed her colours to the poop and sank with the cry, "Long live the Republic!"'

'The *Avenger*,' I cried.

'Yes, the *Avenger*. A glorious name!' the captain murmured, folding his arms.

38

Vengeance

I was strangely moved by this scene, the story begun so coldly, and ended with so much passion, and this name of the *Avenger*, which I felt sure had some particular meaning for the captain. I watched him as he stood gazing at the glorious wreck. Perhaps I should never know his name or his history, but I was beginning to find out what sort of man he was. Some fierce and passionate hatred cut him off from the world, and I wondered whether it might not yet break out in some terrible act of vengeance.

The *Nautilus* rose slowly, and I felt a slight rolling as she surfaced. At once there was a sound like thunder.

'Captain!' I said. He made no answer. I left him and went up on deck, where I found Counsel and Ned.

'What was that?' I said. I looked towards the ship I had noticed before, and saw that she was coming on under full steam, and was only six miles away.

'Gunfire,' said Ned.

'What's that ship?'

'She's rigged like a man-of-war,' he replied. 'I wish she'd sink this damned *Nautilus*!'

'What's her nationality?'

'I can't say. She's flying no flag.'

She drew nearer, vomiting black smoke from her two funnels. Her pennant floated like a streamer, but it was impossible to make out the colours.

'If this ship passes within a mile of us, I'll throw myself into the sea, and you must follow!'

I didn't answer Ned, but went on watching the ship. Whether she were English, French, American or Russian, her crew would certainly look after us if we could get on board. Suddenly a puff of white smoke rose from her bows. A few seconds later there was a great splash astern of the submarine, then the detonation struck my ears.

'They're firing on us!' I cried.

'Good for them!' said Ned.

'But can't they see there are men on board!'

'Perhaps that's why!' said Ned, with a hard look at me.

Of course. The world must know now about the submarine. When we were on board the *Abraham Lincoln* and Ned's harpoon could not pierce the armour-plating, Commander Farragut must have realised what he had been hunting. Now no doubt the *Nautilus* was the quarry of all the warships of the world's navies.

And they had the right, if Captain Nemo had been using her as a means of vengeance! During that night when we were shut up in the cell, he must have attacked some ship, and surely the man who had died had been wounded in the fight. Instead of finding friends in the warship now drawing near, we might well find merciless enemies.

Meanwhile, a rain of shells fell round us, but none hit the submarine. The ship was not more than three miles away, but the captain did not appear.

'Let's signal to them!' cried Ned. 'We must do what we can

to get out of this!' And he took out his handkerchief to wave it in the air. As he did so, he was felled by an iron hand, in spite of his great strength, and sprawled headlong on deck.

'Wretch!' cried the captain in a bellow of rage. 'Do you want me to nail you to the bows of the *Nautilus* before I ram that ship?' His fury was dreadful to witness; his face was white, his pupils narrowed to pin-pricks, he twisted Ned's shoulders under his hands. Then, letting him go and turning towards the man-of-war, whose shells rained round him,

'Ah, you know who I am, ship of an accursed nation!' he cried with his mighty voice. 'I know you though you show no colours! Watch! I'll show you mine!'

And he hoisted a black flag at the bows, like the one he had flown at the South Pole. Then a shell hit the hull, ricocheted past the captain, and buried itself in the sea. He shrugged his shoulders. Then he spoke to me,

'Go below with your friends.'

'Captain,' I cried, 'are you going to attack that ship?'

'I'm going to sink her.'

'You can't do that!'

'I shall,' he answered coldly. 'Don't take it upon yourself to judge me, sir. This is none of your business. I have been attacked, my counter-attack will be terrible. Clear the deck!'

'What ship is she?'

'You don't know? So much the better! You'll never know her flag. Go below!'

We three had perforce to obey. A dozen of the crew were watching the ship's approach with fierce hatred in their eyes. As I went down, I heard another hit on the submarine's hull, and the captain cried,

'Do your worst! Waste your useless shells! You'll not escape the armoured bows of the *Nautilus*. But not here, your accursed hulk shall not be mixed with the glorious *Avenger*!'

I went back to my cabin. The captain and the first officer stayed on deck. I heard the beat of the screw as the submarine withdrew out of range of the warship's guns. The chase continued, the submarine keeping her distance. About four in the afternoon, burning with impatience and anxiety, I went to the ladder. The hatch was open, and I went aloft. The captain was pacing the deck like a wild beast, keeping his eyes on the ship, which was about five or six miles to leeward. He was drawing the pursuer away to the east, but not yet attacking her. Perhaps he was still in doubt. I made up my mind to try for the last time to save the ship, but I had hardly opened my mouth when he stopped me.

'I am justice and human right!' he cried. 'I am the victim, and there is the tyrant! All that I loved, country, wife, children, father, mother, all were destroyed. All that I hate is there! Keep silent!'

I threw one last glance at the ship coming on under full steam, then went to find Ned and Counsel.

'Let's get away!' I said.

'Good,' answered Ned. 'What ship is she?'

'I don't know, but anyway, she'll be sunk before dawn. But I'd rather go down with her than sink her.'

'I agree,' said Ned. 'We'll wait till night.'

Night fell. All was quiet on board. The submarine kept on the surface, holding the same course. We three had made up our minds to jump into the sea as soon as the ship was near enough to hear us or to see us, for it was bright moonlight. We watched our time. Ned wanted to act, but I held him back, for I thought the submarine would attack on the surface, which would make it easy to escape.

At three in the morning, I went up on deck. The captain was still there, standing by his colours, which fluttered over his head.

His eyes never left the ship. He watched her with a strange intensity, seeming to draw her after him with the power of his gaze more surely than if he had her on a tow-line. All was calm and peaceful, the sea was bathed in moonlight. The warship was two miles away, I could see her green and red lights and the white lamp at her mainstay. There were sparks flying up from her funnels as she made full steam.

I stayed on deck till six, without being noticed by the captain. The ship was a mile and a half away, and as day broke she opened fire. It would soon be time for us to jump overboard. I was going below to warn the others when the first officer came up, with several men. The railing round the deck was taken down, the wheel-house and the light-tower were lowered into the hull till they were on a level with it. I went back to the gallery, and found that our speed was slackening. The gunfire sounded louder and shells whistled through the water.

'Now!' I said to the others. We went into the library, but as I opened the door leading to the ladder I heard the sound of the hatch shutting. Ned flung himself on to the ladder, but I stopped him. I could hear the water flowing into the tanks, and in a few minutes the *Nautilus* had dived.

It was too late. The submarine was not going to attack above the water-line, but below, where there was no armour-plating. We were imprisoned again. We went to my cabin, and sat looking at one another in silence, in a sort of frozen horror. We were straining our ears, waiting for a mighty explosion.

We felt the submarine gathering speed, the hull trembled, Suddenly I cried out. There had indeed been a shock, but not violent. There was a grinding of steel against steel, and the *Nautilus* ran straight through the mass of the ship, like a needle through cloth. I rushed like a madman into the gallery. The captain stood silently at the port window, watching the great dark bulk of the ship as she sank. To miss nothing of her agony, the submarine followed her down. Ten yards away, I could see the yawning hole in her side, then the double line of guns. The deck was covered with black running shapes, as the water rose they scrambled up the shrouds, clung to the masts, struggled in the sea.

I watched, dumb with anguish, unable to drag myself from the window.

The great ship sank slowly. Suddenly there was an explosion, blowing up the decks. The *Nautilus* rocked. Then the ship sank more quickly, her rigging came into sight, loaded with men, then the top of her mainmast. Then she was sucked down out of sight, with her drowned crew.

I looked at the captain. That terrible avenger, like an archangel of hatred, still watched. When it was all over, he went to his cabin. Under his gallery of heroes I saw the portrait of a woman, still young, with two little children. He gazed on them for a time, held out his arms to them, then kneeling down he wept bitterly.

39

The Last Words of Captain Nemo

The shutters were closed on the ghastly sight of the sinking ship, but the gallery had not been lighted. Inside the submarine all was darkness and silence. The *Nautilus* was making full speed from the scene of desolation, a hundred feet below the surface. I went back to my cabin, where the other two were still sitting in silence. I could not overcome my horror for the captain; whatever he had suffered at the hands of men, he had not the right to take such a terrible revenge.

At eleven, the lights came on again. I went into the empty gallery, and found that the *Nautilus* was running north at twenty-two knots, sometimes on the surface, sometimes thirty feet below. I saw from the chart that we were passing the opening of the English Channel.

By the evening, we had travelled through two hundred leagues of the Atlantic. I went to my cabin, but I could not sleep and was tormented by waking nightmares. Time passed, but the clocks on board had been stopped and it seemed that night and day no longer followed their appointed course. The earth seemed very far away and I felt I was living in a world of horror and mystery.

I think this northward run must have gone on for about fifteen or twenty days. Neither the captain, nor the first officer, nor any man of the crew was to be seen at any time. The submarine kept submerged, and when she came up for air the hatch was opened and closed automatically. Our position was no longer marked on the chart, and I had no idea where we were.

Ned shut himself up, and Counsel couldn't get a word out of him. Then one morning I woke from a troubled sleep to find Ned leaning over me, speaking in a low voice.

'We're going to escape.'

I sat up. 'When?'

'Tonight. No watch is kept on board any longer.'

'Where are we?'

'In sight of land. I've just seen some coast through the fog, twenty miles to eastward.'

'Right. We'll get away tonight, come what may.'

'There's a strong wind and a rough sea, but we'll take the risk. I've managed to stow some rations and bottles of water in the boat.'

'I'll be with you.' He left me, and I went up on deck. I could hardly stand, but I caught a glimpse of the coast through the eddying fog. Then I went below, to the gallery. I feared and yet wanted to meet the captain once more. It was a long day; at six I dined, without hunger, but wishing to keep up my strength. At half-past six Ned came in.

'Come to the boat at ten,' he said. 'The moon won't be up, it will be dark. Counsel and I will be there.'

I wanted to see our direction, and went to the gallery. We were running north-north-east at a frightening speed, a hundred and fifty feet down. I threw a last glance round the room, with all its treasures, trying to fix it in my memory. Then I went back to my cabin and put on my thickest clothes, tucking the notes of my work inside my jacket. My heart was beating wildly. I wondered what the captain was doing. Next door, in his cabin, I heard him walking up and down. At every moment I thought he was about to come in and ask me why I wanted to leave him. I remembered all I had been through with him, and he seemed to tower above other men, to be a sea-god rather than a human being.

It was half-past nine. Another half-hour to wait! It seemed like eternity. At that moment, I heard soft chords from the organ, a sorrowful harmony stealing through the silence. Then I realised with horror that the captain was no longer in his cabin, but in the gallery which I must cross to escape. A word from him would chain me to the ship for ever. But there was no more time, I had to go. I reached the door of the gallery, and opened it quietly. It was quite dark. The organ still played, but the captain did not see me, and I think that even in daylight he would not have seen me, he was in another world. I tiptoed over the carpet, taking a full five minutes to reach the library door. I was on the point of opening it, when I heard a sigh. A little light filtered through the library door, I saw him stand up. He was coming towards me, silent, his arms folded, moving like a ghost. I heard a sob, then these murmured words:

'Almighty God! Enough! Enough!'

Those were the last words I ever heard from his lips, and it seemed to me that they were a confession of remorse.

I rushed in panic through the library, leapt up the ladder, and ran along the upper passage-way to the boat. I crawled through the hatch, and found the others already there.

'Let's go!' I cried.

'At once!' answered Ned. The hatches were shut and fastened down, and Ned was unscrewing the bolts which still held us to the submarine, when we heard a noise from within. There were voices raised in excitement. Had they discovered our flight? Ned slipped a dagger into my hand.

Then I made out a single word, repeated again and again.

'Maelstrom! Maelstrom!'

Horror struck me cold. Were we then being dragged into that terrible whirlpool on the Norwegian coast, from which no ship has ever come out? I felt the *Nautilus* beginning to turn, then whirling in an ever-narrowing spiral. I was sick with fear and with the violent movement, a cold sweat covered my body.

'We must tighten the screws again!' said Ned. 'If we stay with the ship we may yet be saved . . .'

Even as he spoke the screws gave way, the boat sprang out like a stone from a catapult. My head crashed against the steel frame, and I lost consciousness.

When I came to myself, I was lying in a fisherman's hut in the Lofoten Islands, with my two friends leaning over me. How the boat escaped the Maelstrom I have no idea. We were so happy to be alive, and on dry land. While waiting for a ship, I wrote this story of our adventures.

I have no idea whether they will be believed, though I have written them down carefully, as they happened. I feel that I have now the right to speak of these seas, under which I have voyaged twenty thousand leagues in less than ten months.

But what happened to the *Nautilus*? Did she escape from the Maelstrom, and is Captain Nemo still alive? I hope so, and I hope that he still travels the seas he loves, with all hatred purged from his heart. As for me, I can now truly answer that ringing challenge flung to Job out of the whirlwind: 'Hast thou entered into the springs of the sea? Or hast thou walked in the search of the depth?' Yes, indeed I have – Captain Nemo and I.

THE HISTORY OF VINTAGE

The famous American publisher Alfred A. Knopf (1892–1984) founded Vintage Books in the United States in 1954 as a paperback home for the authors published by his company. Vintage was launched in the United Kingdom in 1990 and works independently from the American imprint although both are part of the international publishing group, Random House.

Vintage in the United Kingdom was initially created to publish paperback editions of books acquired by the prestigious hardback imprints in the Random House Group such as Jonathan Cape, Chatto & Windus, Hutchinson and later William Heinemann, Secker & Warburg and The Harvill Press. There are many Booker and Nobel Prize-winning authors on the Vintage list and the imprint publishes a huge variety of fiction and non-fiction. Over the years Vintage has expanded and the list now includes great authors of the past – who are published under the Vintage Classics imprint – as well as many of the most influential authors of the present.